The Savor
Of The
Salt

The Savor
Of The
Salt

Ione Martens

DAGEFORDE PUBLISHING
Lincoln, Nebraska

ISBN # 0-9637515-1-4
Library of Congress Catalog Card Number: 94-70089

Cover Art by Sally Martens Anderson
        and Angie Johnson Art Productions

Printing by Weber Printing Company, Lincoln, NE

Printed in the United States of America.

DAGEFORDE
Publishing

941 'O' Street, Suite 1012
Lincoln, Nebraska 68508

To my mother, Ruth,
my daughters, Sue and Sally,
and Aunt Mary
who urged me on to completion.

$\mathcal{P}$ reface
&∘⌐

Verses of the Bible invite controversial, or at least, broad interpretations. The King James Version may be even more complex as in this well known verse, Matthew 5:13: "Ye are the salt of the earth, but if the salt have lost his savor, wherewith shall it be salted? It is thenceforth good for nothing but to be cast out, and to be trodden under foot of men."

Substituting flavor for savor helps. If salt were to lose its flavor, it would be worthless. Its purpose would be lost. How then does this apply to people? Could it mean that if people lose their zest for living the good life for which they are intended, they are without value to God and earth?

We know we will fall short of total goodness. Our only hope lies in God's grace to forgive. If we can accept that grace and reconstruct our lives, we need not be cast out. The characters in my story seem to have that understanding.

Ione Martens

Chapter 1

༄ঙ

The square mile country roads were doing their duty. They sectioned off the portions of the earth so it could be properly claimed, and it seemed that all earth was claimed. The ruts in the roads were deep and narrow from wagon wheels homeward bound in recent rains. April green was sprouting even between these tracks in the fertile Nebraska soil. There sat several offspring of these claimants of the earth, resting on their way home from school. High topped shoes nested in the ruts and with arms around knees, the big news of the time was being discussed.

"Halley's Comet means the world's comin' to an end."

"Who says?"

"My dad, and he heard it in town, so it's true."

"How can somethin' just flyin' in the air cause the end of the world?" asked one informed skeptic.

"Well, it's a ball of fire and it could start the world burning. Besides the Bible says the world will end by fire," explains a twelve-year-old authority, standing up and sliding his thumbs under his overall straps.

"Maybe your dad knows a lot, but mine doesn't even know how big my feet are, because these shoes sure do hurt," was the distracted comment from nine-year-old Mary.

"Well the preacher said it too, and he oughta know. He says it has a poison gas that's gonna spread all over and make us sick," piped up another enlightened ten-year-old boy.

"We better get home, 'cause Pop will be mad if we're late," said Mary's younger sister.

"Oh, I have to help with the baby when I get home. Mama says she doesn't know what she'd do without me," says Mary to deaf ears as she remembers responsibilities. Picking up lunch pails, she mothered her two younger sisters onward to the Brown homestead confirming her position as oldest in the family.

That scenario took place in 1910. Halley's Comet came and went and the earth continued to turn. Seventy-six years later it returned and proved to be no threat. The poisonous gas theory did have some scientific merit, but in retrospect, what is amazing is how those ideas were disseminated. Radio and television were not yet invented. Some scarce newspaper or distant chautauqua must have been the news bearers and fear of the unknown was the proliferator.

Chapter 2
∽∽

Forty-five miles across that north-eastern corner of Nebraska was another settlement of earth people whose surnames would most likely be Jones, Morris, Davis, Jenkins, Roberts, Owens, or Evans.

Down the hill from the school was a fine white square house, a newly-constructed gray barn, a red corn crib, and a rapidly turning windmill. Out of the house came nine-year-old Griffith Evans carrying a bucket of ashes to the end of the walk just a few yards from the kitchen door. Dumping them there, spitting and blowing the flying particles off his lips, he skipped back to the house proud to have contributed to the struggling household. They were trying to function without their mother who had passed away two months before. She had been the instigator of the Ladies' Aid at the church just down the road two miles. She and Griffith's dad, Evan, had been born in Wales, but did not meet and marry until after they had come to America. Evan Evans had worked in the iron mills in Gary, Indiana before coming out to Nebraska to buy land. He found his bride among some Welsh settlers in Iowa before coming farther west where those rolling hills seemed to salve some of that latent longing for the homeland. However, he was motivated to be a land owner, as his coal mining predecessors had not been. Success was in his grips, but his partner was gone. There were five healthy Evans children in that household, but there were three infant graves next to their mother in that country cemetery. The three older girls were managing the home. The oldest sister Ferne was in charge, but she was also teaching eight grades at the school up the hill. She was Griffith's teacher. Her twelve years of seniority erased sibling rivalry, and her sense of fairness did not allow for special privilege for her little brother. Griffith's position as "baby of the family" was no longer beneficial. Father Evan administered with a firm discipline and older brother Owen seemed not to serve as a buffer, but instead, a difficult example to follow. Griffith missed his mother's comforting and fending for him in that household of adults.

At the meeting of the Ladies' Aid, Griffith's deceased mother's friends could be heard talking.

"How is little Griffith getting along? He is such a fine little gentlemen."

His wavy hair, high brow, and broad even-featured face evoked pity from these caring women.

They also had concern about Halley's Comet.

"Well, I don't think God has given up on us yet."

"Anyway, we have to get this quilt finished, end of the world or not."

"Pastor Jones tells us to keep our faith and God will take care of us as He does the smallest creature."

"My goodness, we had a good turn-out last Sunday for the Welsh sermon, and I thought some were thinking we shouldn't be having Welsh sermons."

"Well, it doesn't matter in what language we hear the word of God, just so we follow it."

That little church was full every Sunday, and "Blessed Be the Tie That Binds" concluded each meeting. The rich Welsh heritage of being able to and loving to sing was manifested there. No man or horse defied the Sabbath in those hills and vales. No neighbor was left alone in trouble or sorrow. No material possession was arrogantly flaunted. The soil was not exploited. Crops were rotated, and the land was nurtured by products of itself. Still, weeds did grow, and sin was committed. But those Earth People hoed their weeds, looked at their fields and pronounced them "good." The sins were objected to, but the sinners were forgiven by one another and God as their faith had taught them to believe. The salt had its savor. Therein lay the compensation for Griffith's parental deficit.

Chapter 3
❧✕☙

Although a citizen of the same planet, Mary Brown was not so blessed by an aesthetic community spirit. Every March when farmers move, her family was moving. Somehow, her dad Ike would be displeased with his landlord, or more likely, it was the other way around. There would be a new school and different kids to get along with and a new baby at home to help care for.

On one of these new beginnings on a typical windy March day, Mary was told by an older student wishing to intimidate the new girl, "There's an old man with a long beard that comes up from under the bridge to get the girls and take them away."

The "old-too-soon" Mary was consumed by an unconquerable fear for herself and her sisters. Her easy-going, thirty-year-old mother solved the problem by just letting the girls stay home the rest of that year. To make a case of the children's story would seem like trouble-making in a new community, and although a young parent, she had learned not to fight the lifestyle that had become theirs.

Mary learned to sew that year. Time was her teacher and creative tendency her motivator. Of course, there were no yards of lovely new fabrics, but there was a box of used clothing that had been given them. Mary's mother knew how to encourage her.

"Mary go ahead and see if you can make these fit your sisters. I know that you can do better than I can."

By age 15, she was entrusted with new material and kept the females of the family clothed. If commercial patterns were available, she did not use them as she could plan and cut and sew with success and much inner happiness. The treadle of the machine seemed to hum with contentment. There were seven children, only one boy, and Baby Ruth was six months old. Her thirty-three-year old mother caught the measles, unusual but not alarming. Mary was put in charge. Mother could rest and get well, but pneumonia unexpectedly followed and took that young mother from her family. She was buried in a single grave in the cemetery of their town that year, never to be joined by any of her family.

᷾᷾

OBITUARY

Mrs. I. R. Brown died Sunday, April 1916, in her home, at the age of 33 years after a short illness.

The family farmed last year and intended to locate soon in South Dakota, but illness prevented. About two weeks ago the measles epidemic entered the home and the seven children and the mother were attacked by the disease. Mrs. Brown was also taken with pneumonia and her physical strength was not sufficient to bear up under the severe sickness and her tired spirit winged its flight to the world beyond.

Artie May Benson was born March 10, 1883 near Crawford, Indiana, and at an early age united with the Christian Church and by precept and example led the better life she then chose. On July 15, 1900, she was married to Isaac Brown. To them were born eight children, two sons and six daughters, one son dying in infancy.

This death is particularly sad and our people are deeply moved with sympathy for the bereaved family. The oldest is a girl of 15 years and the youngest a babe of six months and to them the kindliest of feelings of our people.

The funeral was held at the Methodist Church Tuesday at 11:00. Rev. C. O. Troudt spoke words of comfort, yet there were few dry eyes as his hearers contemplated the seven motherless children. The body was tenderly laid to rest in the Randolph Cemetery.

This is a copy of the obituary written in that village newspaper. Names have been changed for the purpose of anonymity.

᷾᷾

Life insisted on Mary being strong. N'er-do-well Ike Brown could not keep his family together. The younger girls were "farmed out" to families who could use a little help for their keep. Baby Ruth became the third child of Aunt Grace, her maternal aunt. The three older learned early how to earn board and room, which was not so different except there was no happy, encouraging mother or even a domineering father. Ike even failed at keeping his boy with him. A loving, childless couple took him in. The blood bond was strong and all seven kept in touch.

Mary was adept at earning her way, knowing how to go ahead with duties without explicit directions from the lady of the house. She worked before and after school and on weekends. Going to school was part of the plan with most employers. Also, there was a little money compensation, such as two or three dollars a week. This provided for her clothing and that of the two younger sisters. The need for stamps for all of their letter writing was met by Mary, too. Mary graduated from high school at age 20. This conquest encouraged her to further her education. She matriculated at the Teachers' College, paid fifty cents a college hour, and continued on the work plan that saw her through high school. In one semester she was prepared for teaching but there was no country school needing a teacher. This was no problem as her employer was glad to have her stay on. She could even use the sewing machine.

By the next fall, she was beginning to enjoy some of the benefits of her diligence. Relatives of some of her employers wanted her to teach their school and the Mister was the director so was in charge of hiring. This meant going about 35 miles away from the college town, but she would be closer to the two sisters who perhaps needed her guidance the most. This time she would be paying for her board and room and have money to spare. Life had never been quite so good. The flapper styles were easy to sew, she could buy shoes that fit, and she felt right in her job. Another new joy was the realization that her dark brunette hair, her prominent cheek bones, and her tall slim body drew comments referring to the good-looking, new teacher. Mary had not experienced this before. It seemed that no one had looked, or cared, or she had been into her responsibilities so seriously that she had not listened or heard. Whatever the case might be, she was now enjoying this new popularity. There were plenty of young men home from the war and many who were too young for war but ready for fun in those prosperous, "Roaring Twenties."

The young men were starting to farm and they were buying Model T's. On Saturday nights, they knew the popular
places to go dancing as did the young girls of the area. Mary
was anxious for fun, not responsibility. When her two younger
sisters asked her permission to marry, she realized that she was
viewing marriage as a bondage to work and having babies.

Chapter 4

The biweekly meetings of the Congregational Ladies' Aid were held as religiously as the church meetings. Their concerns marked the passing of time and the trials of the Evans family.

"Is Griffith going to get to finish school?"

"No, the doctor said he'll have to stay quiet for quite a while after that case of blood poisoning."

"Oh well what does it matter if a kid doesn't finish the eighth grade? He's not going to be a doctor, is he?"

"But I think Evan Evans wanted a little more for his children. Ferne was a teacher, you know. Of course she is married now."

"Owen seems to be taking hold and developing into a good farmer."

"Well Evan could show a little more interest in Griffith and the younger girls. Griffith is his baby, after all."

"There might be some drastic changes in the lives of our young men the way that Kaiser Bill is behaving over in Germany."

"That's a long way across that ocean. How many of us ever got over to Wales?"

"Anna Evans did twice. She must have had some power over Evan to get him to spend his money like that."

"He sent her up to Mayo's, too, when she had that problem with kidney stones. Too bad they couldn't save her."

Three years later, only a few meetings had been missed, and most of the same people were in attendance. The President stood to speak.

"We have a thank you note from Evan Evans for serving dinner after Owen's funeral. He enclosed a very generous twenty-five dollar gift. My, he seems so sad; he has endured so much."

"What exactly did happen to Owen?"

"The train whistle frightened his horses right there at the corner of town."

"The horses started running, I suppose?" interjected an anxious listener.

"Yes, he lost control and that load of lumber that he had ended on top of him."

"He was engaged too, wasn't he?"

"Yes, to that nice Morris girl. They say she is just broken hearted."

"Well, I know it's empty consolation, but he won't have to go to war."

The next several meetings were canceled because of the flu epidemic. The community had not experienced illness of this magnitude so they had taken the drastic precaution of canceling.

Griffith and his cousin Irwin were on the Evans' payroll for picking corn. Being speedy paid off. Irwin was one of the fastest pickers around, up to 100 bushels a day. Both of the young men were far behind their usual speed the last several days, as they were not feeling well.

On one of those sunny fall days, Griffith made the suggestion, "Just as soon as we get over the hill, out of Dad's sight, let's stop awhile. I've got to lay down."

Each crawled into his wagon and sprawled over hard ears of corn to rest and soak up healing rays of the sun. This was less than noble behavior, but Griffith had his reasons.

"I don't want to upset Dad. I haven't done anything right since Owen died and now there is Sis's problem too. I wish I could sleep for a week and get over this damned flu. I don't know why Sis got herself in that mess. She sure fell for that line that guy gave her about giving his life for his country."

"What's your dad have to say about that?" asked interested cousin Irwin, knowing his uncle's firmness.

"He's just quiet. Can't tell what he's thinking. I guess she reminds him of Mother. Even now, she can make us laugh once in a while. He's tougher on me, but I can take it better than if she was gettin' it." Griffith was not a big talker, but he was capable of simply stated, endearing sentiments.

Hoping to offer some understanding to his troubled cousin, Irwin said, "You want to go and enlist in the army as soon as we're through picking corn? When I hear that song 'Over There,' I want to go."

"We can't get in the army. We're not old enough."

"I'll bet if we tried we'd make it."

They were seventeen, they tried, but were easily detected when lying about their age. Lies that were told out of wanting to serve their country, have probably been the most forgivable of all falsehoods.

In spite of Griffith's feeling of being out of touch with his dad, he had arranged for him to go to Lincoln to Agriculture School. Evan Evans was often misunderstood because of his non-communicative ways, but he did make caring decisions. This one was probably of a protective nature for his youngest child from some of the grim reality that was to take place. How sad it was that his first grandchild had to be in that stigmatized category of illegitimate. He wondered what the ladies at the Aid meetings would be saying about his family. No doubt he underestimated their compassion.

"Poor girl. No mother all these years."

"Of all the sadness in that family. I wonder how much more he can take."

"Well, she was sowing some wild oats."

"Now, now, we must not cast stones."

"You know she is a lot like our founder, her mother. Always friendly and she sees the bright side of life. If she had had a mother's direction, this wouldn't have happened. Evan couldn't be everything to his family after losing a son."

"They say he just loves that baby girl and sits and rocks her for hours."

"He seems to be a rather gruff man, but he must have a forgiving heart."

The family resumed going to church, the child was taught to behave properly and usually sat by her Grandpa Evans. It must have been then that he took to keeping peppermint candies that came out of his vest pocket with little black fuzzy attachments for which later grandchildren remembered him.

Griffith's session at the Ag School seemed to be creating some changes. His billed cap was worn at a little jauntier tilt, his walk was spirited, and the high, stiff white collars were not so resented. A favorite story he liked to tell about himself concerned a spelling class he was taking. He lacked a natural spelling talent so he memorized a whole list in preparation for the test. The instructor changed the order of the words and he misspelled every one. She thought he needed some extra help and he was eager for the opportunity. Griffith seemed to take a liking to this teacher. Maybe it was that female supervisory attitude that he had been missing in his life.

The Armistice signalled that young men once again make plans for their lives without service interruptions. "Griff" as he was now being called by his peers, became a full-time farmer with his dad. Clear communication between father and son was sadly lacking, but easy-going Griff trusted that his dad knew best and followed his advice. It was easier to do what dad said and have his fun with the other young farmers on Saturday night. One group of which he became a member, called themselves "The Dirty Dozen." They would decide which of the public dance halls they would attend on the next Saturday night, and who would be driving. Evan seemed to be giving Griff a rather free rein in this matter, but was cognizant of the group and that they were all good Welsh farm boys. Their title was "worse than their bite." Prohibition became the law of the land while these young men were exercising their freedom, but it did not seem to make much difference in their activities. Most of them were somewhat financially dependent upon a father who would be against using liquor. It would be difficult to come home in an inebriated condition and still get up early to get chores done before church. Anyway, they were more interested in meeting girls. As this continued for two or three years, nature and family background changed their hunting. It became "wife hunting." The criteria for wives became "good mothers for their children." Most of society may be better off because of the change in this pursuit.

The Crystal Ballroom near Wisner had reached new heights in the numbers drawn there. Some of Griff's old gang had already taken the big step; but a few were still in earnest about finding their conquests for life. They did think that way despite the hedonistic spirit that seemed to dominate the "Twenties." Perhaps that is attributable to the savor of the salt at that time and place.

Chapter 5
ᕯᕮᕲ

Because of Supreme planning, young popular women also change. Mary Brown had tired a little of similar approaches, aggressive passes, flirtatious lines, non-committal conversation and insincerity, in general. She knew she had invited this behavior by her somewhat caustic remarks about marriage. She still liked to dance and hoped someone different might come along. If not, she could "kid around" with the stand-bys who were always good for a dance or two. For three years, she had taught in that same rural school and boarded in the same home, so life was quite stable just a few miles from Wisner and the Crystal Ballroom.

Although it was appropriate for a young woman to go to these dances unescorted, they were insistent upon introductions to new dance partners and their names must be written upon the lady's dance card. Incidentally, the Crystal charged admission to the men only, no doubt based on the tenet that the men would go where the women could be found.

Griff inquired about a dark-haired woman whom he noticed but had not connived an introduction. He had alerted his cohorts to help him in this, since he was attracted by the fact that she was usually dancing, laughing and seeming to have a good time. She did not act as though she was "sweet on" anyone in particular. She was slim, and while Griff was not a student of fashion, she reminded him of the girls he admired when he was in Lincoln at the University. His friend George came to his rescue.

"Griff, I have everything under control. Come over there with me and I'll introduce you to that girl you've had your eye on. I found out she is a teacher. Your 'old man' would like that."

That was both pleasing and intimidating news. Thoughts of his spelling handicap were painful, but that teacher at Ag School seemed to kind of like him. They were crossing the room and it was happening.

"Mary Brown, I want you to meet Griffith Evans." He had warned George not to use his whole name, but George had his own brand of orneriness when he was doing a favor.

The first sound out of Mary was a warmhearted giggle, and then "Hello, it is nice to meet you. My that is a dignified sounding name. I would be real proud to have that on my dance card."

She was making things easy for him and actually he liked the friendly ribbing, besides it was taking up those first awkward moments. She deserved his newest practiced line, "Say, that dress is the cat's meow."

She had heard that one before, but smiled and liked his effort at being sophisticated. That's what she had been trying to be when she copied the dress from a picture in a newspaper.

He decided that whole name business wasn't so bad after all. As he wrote it on the dance card, she watched and he felt that she would never forget his name.

When his turn to dance with Mary came, he was there waiting as she came off the dance floor with her previous partner. She wasn't listening to him so much as she was smiling at Griffith, liking his innocent face. She felt older because of his boyish charm, but didn't she always? Between her "oldest in the family" attitude and her "teacher in charge" feeling, how could she not feel that way? He danced well and led strongly. That helped diminish some of her "in charge" feeling.

He was glad she started the conversation.

"Do you always ask older women to dance?"

"You're not older than I am," he responded naturally and straight forwardly.

"Oh," was all it took from her to find out what she wanted to know.

"I'm a year younger than this century."

She thought that was a clever way of putting it. He did too. She could see that she did not have to be cagey to elicit information from this clean-cut, good-looking man.

"I am too," she replied.

Birthday information was exchanged and she was an older woman by two months. Both egos were satisfied, both hearts were stirred.

For several Saturday nights, it was agreed that they would see each other the following week with no specific dates made.

Mary was somewhat disappointed as she had sensed more than a casual friendship had begun. Griff was afraid to make a date and not be able to keep it because of bad roads or some demands that his dad might ask of him. This was something that he could not easily voice as it sounded "unmanly." Pride was their enemy. Mary had to show him a little less attention. That was much safer than rejection. She resumed her former pattern of keeping a full dance card. If Griff cared, he would have to take some overt action. She knew this innately, and he came to realize it. He made dates and kept them. He drove to the home where she boarded, took her to the dance, and took her home in a respectable fashion. She was his girl by his definition. However, there had been no such proclamations or proposals made.

Chapter 6
❧❧

It was a day in March that had a hint of Spring in it that prompted Griff to do the chores early and drive thirty miles to see his girl in the middle of the week. He was sure that would please her as she had teased him about never doing anything on "the spur of the moment." Driving into the farm yard, he saw two other cars, only one of which he recognized as Mary's sister and her husband's. He felt tinges of discomfort, thinking he might be intruding on some gathering. He went to the house and there he saw his competition. He made his usual greetings to the people of the house, and then they retreated to the kitchen, leaving the parlor to the young people. Mary's sister who was a fixer, either by nature or position in the family, was contriving a plan to solve the situation of two boyfriends, one girl, and no date set by either. While Mary was making awkward conversation, she rushed into the kitchen to pull a straw from the broom and broke it into long and short pieces.

"I know what we can do. We'll just have you two guys draw straws to see who gets the date with Mary," holding up her hand with only ends of the straws evenly displayed.

Grabbing that hand, not harshly but firmly, Griff said, "I didn't drive thirty miles to draw straws. I came here to see Mary and this other fellow better be on his way." Most easy-going people have that point beyond which they will not be pushed.

"Sorry Fellah, didn't know anybody had any claims on her. See you around, Mary."

Mary was awe-struck. Griff's authoritative behavior was creating new thoughts and feelings. "No one has ever claimed me like this before. I like him taking charge. He seems to want me, not just exercise power over me."

"Well, we better be going. Nice to see you again, Griff." Mary's sister and brother-in-law liked Griff but had not taken him as a serious suitor any more than any other of Mary's friends.

Soon they would be alone and Mary would have to deal with this revelation of new realizations. "I didn't know we had a date." She was being defensive in spite of the rush of respect she was feeling for Griff. She wanted to be warm and docile, but this was not a practiced art with Mary.

"No, we did not have a date, but I sure thought you were my girl and that I could count on you to be loyal."

"I can give up that fellow and some others, too, if I know why I'm doing it," came pouring out of the mouth of this strong-willed woman who had never needed anyone. Her wanting to be claimed had been hidden even from herself.

"I been thinking, and I want you to be my wife. Is that a good enough reason?"

"That is a very good reason, and I think I would like that, but there are many things to talk about before we do anything rash." This probably wasn't the passionate response he wanted to his proposal, but it had not been very romantically given.

Now that Mary and Griff were marriage bound and their hearts were attune, conversation changed to planning. That is the glorious power of commitment. Frivolous talk was out. Clever repartee was not necessary. They need to talk about how many children they would have. Mary stood firmly on not having one child after another, although birth control measures were not yet invented nor was the subject publicly discussed. Then there was a matter of names for the boy and girl that would make up their little family. They would live on the "home place" since Griff was the only living son, and eventually they would be owners of the farm. Although Griff would never brag of comfortable wealth, he was quite confident that they could have the good life. He wanted his wife to go to Ladies' Aid and be active in the church. Naturally, this was how he viewed the woman's place even though he had only nine years while his mother was living. While he was stating his expectations, Mary was being won over. Family stability, land of their own, and being accepted in a church and community sounded Heaven sent.

"Maybe your church won't like me because I'm not Welsh," Mary worried.

"Those ladies have always been nice to me, and have been teasing me about when I was going to bring a bride to church. The way you sew and all, I'll bet you can quilt and that's what they do at all their meetings." Griff was not the romantic type, but he certainly knew how to ease Mary's mind.

"Now you know we'll have threshers to feed every summer. That's a bunch of hungry men to feed. Can you make pies?"

"Anything in the cooking department doesn't worry me. Most of the people I worked for liked what I cooked," she assured him. "What about you? Are you fussy?"

"I like everything, especially meat, mashed potatoes and gravy. Sis was a pretty good cook, but since she got married, Dad and I just batch and that isn't so good. It will be nice to have a woman in the house again."

"What about your dad? Where will he live?" asked Mary a little unnerved by this last information.

Griff had been avoiding this subject. As naive as he was, he knew that newlyweds liked being alone in their new domain.

"Well, he will have to live with us since it is his farm and there is no place else for him to go." Griff tried to appeal to her logic and sympathy. "It's a big house and he'll be so glad for your cooking, he won't give you any trouble."

Mary's misgivings were short-lived and other more important things had to be planned. "When shall we get married? I'll have to finish out the year teaching, so that would mean no sooner than May."

"That would be a pretty good time — toward the end of May so I could be through with corn planting and I could send some cattle to market so I would have some extra money for a honeymoon."

Now she liked what she was hearing. Her heart warmed to this gentle, honest, uncomplicated man.

"You won't last until May if I don't leave so you can get to bed. You have to teach tomorrow."

Mary knew she would not sleep much after all the excitement. It seemed to be natural for a teacher to plan and she could revel in it. Love is the enhancement of each tomorrow.

Chapter 7

On their regular Saturday night dates, Mary and Griff went dancing either to the Crystal Ballroom or to some other place where the crowd would be going. It was the custom to exchange dances with other couples and the remaining bachelors from "The Dirty Dozen" danced with Mary to make sure Griff was getting a good woman. Their introducer always had to tease, to make sure that she preferred Griff over him. After each dance evening, they would talk, for there was much to learn about each other.

"Since your mother died so young, what has your dad been doing? You never mention him," asked Griff.

"What's more, I don't intend to. He did not do one thing to help us kids after Mom died. He couldn't even keep my brother. I've lost track of him and that suits me just fine."

Griff detected a lot of bitterness in what Mary said and decided he would not bring up that subject again. Mary was glad that the truth had come out as she had worried some about her lack of family background.

This seemed an appropriate time for Griff to tell about his sister and her baby. He was relieved as Mary seemed sympathetic. She was. She had known girls who would go away for a while and be different when they came back home. She had been particularly suspicious of a friend's offer to go away with her. Her dad was willing to pay all expenses. She resisted the invitation, mostly by an intuitive hunch. Later, she heard this girl had gone away to have an abortion. She had worried about her two closest sisters, but they were both married and each had their first child. She knew that girls without strong family ties were regarded as "easy marks." Mary and Griff vowed that they would not spoil their lives like that.

On another evening during an exchange of vital information, the location of the farm where Mary and Griff would be living came up. Mary realized, "That can't be very far from where my mother is buried."

"That's about ten miles from home. Good, then we can go and visit her grave at times when you want to," was Griff's natural response.

Mary was touched anew by this man's tenderness.

"I want to take you to the farm and meet my family, but I don't see how I can come down here and get you, take you there, and then get you back here in one day before we get married."

"Yes, I'm anxious to meet your family too, but I do see the difficulty. I'm so glad you like my sisters and they like you. I wasn't so sure after the drawing straws incident," and they laughed together remembering it as one of their precious moments.

"I'll see you next week. And do you realize that will be May, 1924, the month we get married?" Griff extoled.

"Yes, I have three more weeks of school. I think everybody will pass this year. I'll have to tell them I'm not coming back, and then I need to shop for a new dress. I want a readymade dress to get married in."

They hated to part, but practicality won.

Chapter 8

May arrived. Mary and Griff were joyous with their weekly reunion. Griff reported progress of the field work. Mary was carrying out responsibilities. They went to the dance. Their chums had caught on to their special feelings and were teasing them about "tying the knot." Of course, they denied any plans since it was much more exciting to have the deed done before anyone knew except for those standing up with them. Both were enjoying being suspect and maintaining intrigue. It was their secret from the world.

Closeness and understanding had reached a high peak. They felt as though their dream of marriage had already become a reality. Further talking was not needed. The May midnight was ethereal. Passion won.

Chapter 9
∽◦∾

Telephone lines were strung on low poles through this part of the country, and they were owned by private individuals or companies that maintained a central operator who made the connections for each local call or to another central for a long distance call. The subscribers to this service often had to go out and put up the wires after a wind or ice storm. There was very little privacy in this system as each home phone would ring for any call on that particular line. There were usually ten or twelve parties on one line. Each had a certain combination of long and short rings to designate when that party was being called. All on the line knew when anyone was called or when anyone called Central to make any other call. Common courtesy was the only defense of privacy and we know how curiosity can offset that. Griff knew well the limitations of the telephone so on the first Saturday of the May rains, he did not call Mary as he was sure she would understand why he could not get there to see her. The next week, conditions were no better so he called but did not want to give away their secret plans. The conversation was unsatisfactory.

"Mary, I can't make it down there on these roads."

"No, I suppose not. When will I see you again?" Mary was aware of restrictions of their conversation, but wanted to shout "What about our marriage plans?"

"I'm way behind in corn planting because of these rains," trying to relay that their plans would have to be put off until the planting was done.

"School's out, you know. I'll leave my things here, but I don't board here over the summer. I suppose I should look for a summer job." Mary was seeking answers but knew she was not going to get any under the circumstances.

"How am I going to know where you'll be?" Griff was beginning to feel unsure of everything.

"I suppose I can write a letter if you really do want to keep in touch," said Mary, probing but hurting.

"Well, sure I do." He detected her doubts but couldn't say the right thing. "Well, goodbye."

Could this be the same couple who were ecstatic over wedding bells two weeks ago?

Mary felt let-down, hurt, frightened, angry and alone. Sadness consumed her thoughts. "Why does life have to be so cruel to me? I'm 23 years old and nothing is any easier than when I was 15 and Mama died. Why do I believe anything any man tells me? They're all the same. They just want their way with a woman then drop her. Why can't I read character better? I really thought Griff was different, but he isn't. He even scared off my other boyfriends. What will I do about a job? I told the school board that I had been here long enough so did not want to sign a contract for next year. I suppose I could still have it, but they would figure out that my boyfriend had dropped me. I'm not letting anyone think that. Wonder what I could find in Lincoln? I could get there on the train. I'm sure not going to be available. If Griff is sincere, he will have to prove it by coming a long ways to see me." As she dealt with her pain, she came to some resolve. The idea of going to Lincoln even had some excitement about it as she had never been to any big city. "Griff had almost been smug about his time in Lincoln, and if he could get around there, she could too." She had saved money regularly, having decided a few years ago that she never wanted to be totally without money again.

Mary's landlord took her to the train station in Wisner, saw her off with much hand-waving and good-luck-wishing. They had become sincere, caring friends, almost family. She easily found a room to rent because of the university situation, and the next day started the job search. Although, women by that time had received the franchise to vote, there were definite limitations on types of jobs. She did find a job cleaning tables and doing dishes at the university cafeteria. She had to remind herself that this was just a summer job and that she was cleaning up after nice people. Mary appreciated her career as a teacher more each day. She realized that she had risen above some levels of life because of her own determination and maybe fate had been a little kind. Morale was improving. She could still attract young men and accepted a few dates. This was the time she missed Griff the most. It had been easy to be with him from the beginning and their recent good times had the excitement of looking to the future and now that was gone. He had said to let him know where she went so he could get in touch with her. But maybe he didn't mean that either. Well, she would never know if she did not give him a chance. She would have to construct a letter very carefully. If he were backing out on the marriage plans, she did not want to hear the awkward truth. All he had to do was ignore her letter. She must not relay to him any feelings that she had one way or the other. A smart woman gives a man a chance to get out; otherwise, she never knows if his attention is interest or obligation.

Dear Griff,

I am in Lincoln as you can see by my return address. It's exciting being in the city with many places to go and people to meet. I can see why you liked it when you were here. My job is not great, but is alright for a temporary job. Annie and Gus took me to the train and the ride was fun.

I suppose you are caught up on your work by now and probably have been down to the Crystal Ballroom. Tell the old gang "Hi" for me.

Always, Mary

Evan Evans picked up the mail the day that casual letter arrived. Tossing it to Griff when he came in for supper that night, he said "looks like that school teacher's fancy handwriting. Haven't heard you say anything about her lately."

Griff was trying to seem calm in front of his dad, but his heart was vibrating his whole body. He couldn't open the envelope in front of his dad. That would be exposing his life, and they had not overcome their communication barrier. He went out to the front porch to read. Besides he wanted to be alone with Mary. The letter did not serve that wanting. He could see that she had not understood him. Even when one is to blame for being misunderstood, it is a hurting feeling. His impulse was to drive to Lincoln, but that was 175 miles one way. That was difficult to justify to his dad and would take too many arrangements. Heaven knows the telephone wasn't the answer. He would have to write a letter and soon.

"Oh boy, I've got my work cut out for me. I would rather plow a field than write a letter and spell all those words. Sure glad I told Mary about my problem. Maybe she will understand that one, but she doesn't sound like she is very interested in what I might have to say." There was no alternative, it had to be done.

Dear Mary,

I was very glad to here from you. No I have not gone to the crystal. I would not go without you. Did you forget are plans. I love you I want to marry you.

Love, Griff

To speed the letter on its way, he went to town the next morning on the pretense of needing to get parts to fix the binder. It would be small grain harvest time soon.

Chapter 10
❧

Mary had worked the lunch and dinner shift for the first time since she had asked for the change from the breakfast schedule, when she came home to the miracle of miracles, a letter from Griff. She dropped into a chair and held it unopened for a moment. Was this going to be an answer to a problem or the end of hoping for an answer? She could scan the short letter quickly, but she was treasuring every word. She smiled at his errors, knowing how he had struggled. The smile lingered but her eyes moistened and salty droplets passed over her lips. He was saying what she desperately had to know. Her response would be like his, open and without caution.

My Dear Griff,

Your letter was here today when I came home from work. It made me very happy, because I had given up hope that you wanted our dreams to come true. I haven't forgotten one word of what we talked about and yes, I still want to be your wife.

The one remaining problem is that you did not mention when we could be married. I could not survive setting a date again and being disappointed. Will you please not let that happen? You better tell your dad as the shock may be too much for him and I think it may be a little more pleasant for me. Since he will be living with us, best he and I get off to a good start.

I do not need to worry about giving notice with this job as it seems there are different people on the job every day.

It's good to be planning and to be excited about life again. I love you.

Mary

It would be a classic understatement to say Griff was a happy man when he received this letter. He momentarily worshipped the written word. He began a pattern of behavior that existed for years to come. He followed Mary's suggestions. He was eager to please. Perhaps, part of the attraction of one person to another is based upon unrecognized needs that begin in childhood. Griff, being the baby of his family, seemed to need direction given to him. Mary, as eldest in her family, tended to give instruction as a natural way of life. Surely, they never talked about this but it became an attribute to their relationship.

"Dad, I want to talk to you about getting married," said Griff in his newly-mustered courage.

"I'm not getting married," replied Evan Evans purposely making it more belabored.

"I don't mean you, I mean me."

"Plenty young. How are you going to support a wife?" He knew how Griff would answer the question but wanted to hear the answer that showed reliance on him.

"Gosh, Dad, I thought that was what you wanted me to do. Get married and settle down to full-time farming. That's exactly what I have in mind, and my girl does, too."

"Who is this girl? Anybody I know or know of? Where is her family from?"

"Her name is Mary Brown and the only family she has are sisters." Griff thought about adding that her dad used to be a farmer, but he knew the next question would be about his present whereabouts, so he avoided bringing it up.

"Humph, sounds funny to me. Even sounds like a made-up name."

"Well, I haven't met any Welsh girls any nicer or prettier or who can do all the things Mary can. Besides, she is a teacher and you always thought that was the greatest thing a girl could do when Sis was my teacher." Griff's defensiveness was showing, and it was also making a little inroad in his dad's thinking. He was proud that he had stood up to his dad. It may well have been that this was all a part of Evan Evan's technique in training a son.

"Well, you know that I plan to stay right here in this house, don't you?"

"Yes, I understand that, but you have to give her a chance and you'll like her." Griff knew this was as much of a concession as he would get so was satisfied with having prepared his dad as Mary had suggested.

Now he had to write another letter. He sure would be glad when they were married so he wouldn't have to write letters, although he was gaining some confidence in the results.

Dearest Mary,

I talked to Dad like you suggested and he is all set for me to bring a wife here to live. I hope that makes you feel better.

I think a good time to get married would be the first Wednesday in August. I will leave here early in the morning so we can go to the court house in the afternoon. Can you get someone from there to stand up with us? We will go on our honeymoon from there. We will come back up north because I here the Yankton bridge will be open. That way we will see something new like us and see if it lasts as long as we do. I'm sure excited about being your husband so I can look out for you and you won't have to work again.

Love, Griff

Just as a teacher analyzes a student's homework, Mary thought as she read this last letter over and over, he certainly did follow instructions. He told his dad and set a date. I think it will work out this time. Old doubts and tenseness did not allow her to be as joyous as she expected to be. She did like the honeymoon ideas and his sentiment about it. She just hoped she felt good enough.

That night in bed, when it's easier to deal with one's shortcomings, Mary cried in her pillow and then slid out of bed directly to her knees and prayed. Still hugging the pillow, she thanked the Good Lord for intervening in her life. She hadn't always felt so cared for, but, in this most frightening time of her life, she was grateful. She consoled herself that it might even mean forgiveness of sin. She would never have used the secret to get Griff to marry. Her true happiness was based on the faith that God had put her in the hands of a good and sincere man.

Chapter 11

The Yankton Bridge was officially declared open for traffic and Mary and Griff were officially husband and wife. Griff would have to know their deeper bond soon. The opportunity arrived when he remembered her wishes concerning too many babies too fast.

"I want you so much, but will you be mad at me if you get pregnant right away?"

"Well, we won't have to worry about that for awhile. I already am. Remember that beautiful night in May when we felt married."

"Oh no, Honey, and you had to worry about that all by yourself and find a job. I'm so sorry. I should have been right there beside you. I'll make it up to you."

"I did not know what I was going to do," and she wept. She knew most men would have felt tricked and would have doubted her statement. Again she felt grateful.

They drove into the farm yard late on Sunday night. Evan had gone to bed so she did not meet him until the next morning. She did not get to see the house or farmstead that night. Griff led her upstairs to his room. Evan slept downstairs so she felt more like a stowaway in her new home than a celebrated bride.

What a difference a ten-minute marriage service makes in young lives. The newlyweds get up in the morning and it was suddenly acceptable that they slept together, very likely in a bed that they wanted to share much earlier but would not dare. However, the sort of nervous embarrassment is still there. Here in particular, Griff knew he did not have an easy task. He had practiced the introduction in silence and his dad was more congenial than usual. Maybe the old man had some romance in his soul after all. The two men showed Mary the whole farm with great pride. Here in 1924, they had saved five acres of prairie hay. That section of soil had never been tilled, and Griff well understood that he would expect to maintain his dad's example. They showed her the mulberry trees that just grew and the cherry orchard that was carefully planted.

Evan broadly hinted, almost playfully, "Those cherries sure do make good pie filling in a good crust."

Griff was confident his bride would prove herself well.

"Say, you two better be getting spruced up, because in about an hour this yard is going to be filled with our neighbors to wish you well."

Mary and Griff looked at each other recording a pleasant surprise. At this moment, Griff felt mighty proud of his dad.

Mary quickly asked, "Will they expect to see us in our wedding clothes?"

"Well sure, that's what we're celebrating."

She checked the condition of her hair and decided her marcel was still holding so it would not be necessary to heat up her curling iron. And then, her first bath in her new home. The bathroom was exactly that, a room with a bathtub. The water was not running but was close at hand as it would be drawn from the water reservoir on the cook stove. It would not be real warm since a fire had not been burned since early morning. It meant a trip from here to the upstairs bedroom to dress. Mary did not regard this as an inconvenience. Actually, she was impressed with the permanent tub facility.

Both dressed excitedly, Mary asking if she looked alright and Griff assuring her that she was pretty but not wasting words in lavish praise.

Soon the yard was full of "tin lizzies" and uproarious noise makers such as sticks pounding on buckets and cow bells shaking violently. Mary was glad to see several familiar faces, those of the "Dirty Dozen" who could make it to this shivaree. They did not know the origin of the custom, but they knew it meant acceptance and they were glad.

After the noisy part was over, warm greetings were extended to the new bride and congratulations to Griff on his choice. While they looked over the new woman, it was not an unkind scrutiny. They wanted her to fit in as much as she wanted to.

With much ado, ice cream was created with pounding of blocks of ice, pouring the proper amount of salt, and turning the crank until the contents of the freezer were solid. The men, of course, took care of this while the women were cutting the fluffy, frosted cakes that they had brought. The refreshments became the entertainment. No wedding reception ever included a happier bride and groom. At the next meeting of the Ladies' Aid, a healthy check went into the treasury from Evan Evans for the happy festivities.

Chapter 12

Female-type changes were taking place at the Evans farmstead. Crisp curtains were visible through shining windows. Linoleum floor covering was scrubbed clean. Although too late for flower planting this year, beds were prepared. A fence was put up around the yard, and the ash pile at the end of the sidewalk was hauled off by wheel barrow. Mary was at the helm in all of these activities, with Griff and Roy, the new hired man, taking the orders. This created some of the first marital discord. They laughed and had a good time about the ashes as Griff remembered taking them out there, and now with a woman in his life that all changed. He wondered why they never bothered anyone before, but was glad for the improvement. Roy saw it as an opportunity to tease Griff.

"Boy Griff, you sure can see who wears the pants in your family." This hateful cliché bothered Griff.

"Well, Mary has some good ideas and the place sure looks better."

"Yeah, that's true but the way she gives the orders is what I'm talking about. She sure wants to make a slave out of you."

"If you want to keep on working here, you'd better stay out of my business. And besides, I don't like the way you compliment Mary's cookin' all the time." Griff felt he stood up to Roy like a man, but it hurt him to know another young man viewed his marriage that way. He would have to talk to Mary about this.

Mary didn't like the idea that Griff was so worried about the hired man's opinion and that he had talked to his boss that way. And as for the compliments, "You never give me any, so you don't want him to either."

This went on record as their first quarrel. It had all the necessary qualities.

Love worked its magic after a little coolness. Roy did stop the compliments so Griff regained status. When Mary chided him about not complimenting her, his reply was always, "Well, I'm eating it." It became an understood joke between them and for many years Griff could often be heard repeating it followed by a laugh.

Threshing had been finished before they were married, which alleviated some stress for the new bride, but the curse of living at the home place effected its pain. Family from Iowa arrived to visit, probably cordially invited by Evan, but unbeknownst to Mary. There were several beds to be made and endless meals to prepare for their week's stay. Mary was tiring easily at this time, but keeping the secret and courageously carrying on. Griff was somewhat helpful, but his work and chores went on, too. Evan had become convinced that Mary could do anything. Mary thought as many strong women have thought, "I'd be better off if I let them down once in a while." Finally, the day of departure came. They waved them out of the yard until out of sight. Mary sat down exhausted. Strength had not even begun to return, when voices were heard, "The front axle broke on the car and they will have to order one. Looks like we'll be staying another week."

Mary always wondered what kept her from fainting. That night came the breakdown. She cried and told Griff she didn't think she could go on.

Griff had no solution to the problem, but he did understand. Somehow, this man of few words, found some to attempt to soothe his wife. "I know how hard this is on you, but you have been doing so well. I wish it didn't have to be this way. We shouldn't be living here with my dad anyway. None of this is fair to you." He held her tight and the sobbing diminished and ended. She had been understood and respected.

Griff came through this crisis much better than he did in their first quarrel. He relayed genuine sympathy, and maybe there is something to the idea that love will show the way and each time that it works for the couple, they are wiser and stronger in their faith in love.

Chapter 13

The "Twenties" were prosperous. However, the way that Mary and Griff experienced it was vastly different than the lifestyles portrayed by F. Scott Fitzgerald, the popular author of that time. These Nebraska farmers enjoyed a good price on the cattle they took to market. Mary and Griff worked out a system. Mary would decide which household item was most needed and each time there was some income from the cattle sales, it could be purchased. Of course, there were many other needs to be considered. The oven door on the cookstove would not stay tightly closed and a few baking failures were close to causing some crises. This became a top priority. A "Kopper Klad," one of the best on the market, became an object of pride and satisfaction. Mary's way of showing delight with the new purchase was natural and very smart. She kept her stove top shining by sanding it regularly with an emery cloth on a brick, and the bread and cakes were the results of an expert. The latter probably impressed Griff and his dad the most. The next major improvement was a Maytag washer with a gasoline motor and a roller wringer. Mary would heat the water in the big oval boiler before cooking breakfast. Then Griff helped put the water into the washer and start the engine on the washing machine before starting his farm work for the day. A woman's pride lay in the whiteness of her wash that hung to dry in the bright sunlight. Somehow, neighbors knew which women did not put out a white wash. Many of them, including Mary, made their own soap. This process usually accompanied butchering, which meant rendering lard, some of which would be for the soap. Lard would be stored in stone crocks in the cave deep in the ground. Hams were rubbed with curing salt and when a cow was butchered, meat was actually canned in glass jars. This was the most readily available meat for unexpected company and always delectable with its juices made into gravy. Women of that time, although they didn't use the word, certainly knew fulfillment. They could look around and see their accomplishments.

Chapter 14
❧

It was the regular meeting of the Ladies' Aid in February 1925. Visiting was best done bent over a quilt that was on frames, one hand under the quilt to push the needle back to the topside to make another stitch.

"So, Mary and Griffith have a baby boy. Isn't that grand. I think it's extra nice when the first one is a boy," stated one of the faithful matrons.

"He is a little mite, but just as healthy as can be, at least, that's what Doc Ackerman said," reported another.

"Well, they have been blessed. Any healthy child is a blessing," said an older member almost as a ritual.

A younger matron dared to breach the subject others were avoiding. "The baby is small, but he came a little too soon, didn't he?"

"I don't count months, but it doesn't seem they have been married very long. Let's see when was it we had the lawn party for them?"

"Now, now, ladies we must not pass judgment. That's usurping God's power," was the good advice from the minister's wife.

"That's true and all of us here are married women and we know men can be ever so kind and gentle, but they expect their rewards. And if we didn't have a baby too soon, it's just because God gave us some extra strength," offered a younger, less suppressed woman.

"I certainly agree with that and yet we women get the blame for Adam's fall. That part of the Bible has always bothered me," said an older woman not known as a dissenter before this moment.

The president decided this was a good time to shift to the business part of the meeting and safe subjects such as treasurer's reports and the like.

Mary and Griff, named their first born Owen after Griff's deceased brother which pleased Evan and the one requirement that Griff made was it had to be an easier name than his. Mary made no mention of using her father's name.

With each day of baby raising, there are dozens of lessons on parenting. First children everywhere seem to feel their parents learn all they know at their expense. Being a parent is probably the most demanding activity that people get into and yet the one for which young people are the least prepared. Here too, love and faith seem to see the young parents through and the children blossom and grow.

Chapter 15
ᔧᕈ

The busiest grocery store in town was sponsoring a contest to win a radio. The craze to have a headset was sweeping the country. It had taken a little time as the first radio broadcast went on record as being in 1921. The winning set was displayed right there in the store which included a box or receiver and headgear which was placed over the ears so only one person could hear at a time. By whatever method the winner was determined, Mary was the lucky one. She was thrilled with the prize but hardly had time to sit and listen. Rather than let it sit and not get used, Evan in his practical way, tried it out. His age excused him from the farm work so he did have the time. At times, Mary begrudged him this joy but it became a blessing. Little Owen was an active child, so quite regularly, Evan would cajole him into sitting on his lap and listen to the sounds coming from the ear coverings. Often Owen would fall asleep and Evan felt justified in his takeover of Mary's radio.

In just a little over two years, Owen had a baby sister. She arrived with little fanfare, her mother's equanimity, her father's joy, and no gossip. She was named Sarah Ruth and her disposition seemed to match her entrance into this world. It was a blessing that she was easy to care for, since two-year-old Owen was a mischievous dynamo. Mary and Griff felt life was being good to them as their children were healthy and they had the ideal family.

The most recent furniture addition was a lovely oak dining room table and chairs with a matching buffet in the "Queen Anne" style. The dining room was a large 16-foot square room. It was meant to be the biggest room in the house since eating was such an important activity. Mary was very protective of the new furniture, but she did allow Owen to ride around the center table on his tricycle. Because of the attention given to the new baby and many admonitions, Owen's naughtiness exuded.

One morning, Mary was bathing the baby, thinking Owen was playing peacefully, when she heard the noise of much breaking glass. She hurriedly wrapped the soap-slippery baby in a towel and ran to the dining room. By this time, the naughty two year old was running his tricycle over the already broken china which he apparently had dragged out of the lower shelves of the buffet. He was squealing with joy. Mary yelled at him to stop this minute and threatened him with "Wait until your father sees this mess." She knew that Griff was working out in the corn crib so she went to the door and yelled for him to come in at once. She saw this as a major disciplinary matter. Alarmed at these unusual circumstances, Griff rushed to the house. Mary pointed to the dining room and there Griff saw the catastrophe with a crying little boy covering his eyes and a tricycle sitting in the midst of broken china. His very first reaction was relief there was no blood and next was a short muted laugh — that of a father a little amused at his tough little boy. Mary's face and words indicated no amusement, "I can't be the only one to make these kids behave. Of the few times I have called you to help and you have laughed. You expect me to make all the decisions and be firm and cross with them and you do nothing. What kind of a father are you?" She was screaming by this time and Griff felt persecuted. He responded with the cruelest of all words.

"For all I know I might not even be this kid's father."

Mary retreated to care for the baby, drying tears with the baby towel. Griff knew the hurt that he had perpetrated, but there was no apology forthcoming. He started the clean up and told Owen to get the broom. Even the two year old sensed the tension and eagerly obeyed.

Supper was prepared as usual, however, the little family and Grandpa were very quiet. Suddenly Griff spoke.

"Dad, I think things would work out better if we moved up to the place by Sholes and one of the girls and their families came and stayed here with you."

"What makes you think that?" was Evan's natural response.

"I can't do anything to please you, and Mary and I aren't getting along very well."

"What makes you think it will be any better on another farm?" Evan did ask hard questions.

"Well, don't blame Mary. I'm the one who's cross and crabby."

Mary was sitting there in awe of what Griff was saying. In a way it sounded as though he was making excuses for his harsh words. On the other hand, he was trying to do something about the problem and being more direct with his dad than ever before. She didn't know that Griff had been so bothered by his dad's supervision. She reasoned that they hadn't had much time to talk because of the baby and the everyday business of living. Responsibility takes a toll on young parents.

"Maybe I made a mountain out of a molehill. Owen is only two and he hasn't been getting the attention he wants. He wasn't being spiteful. I should have just given him a spanking and been done with it," Mary thoughtfully lamented.

Mary was so encouraged with Griff's talk with his dad, that she could admit to getting too angry over the incident, but she defended herself on the basis that a woman doesn't have as much self-control for a while after having a baby. Griff admitted that the dining room was quite a sight, and any parent would be very upset. There was a little easing of the tension but no quick kissing and making up.

A pattern of behavior was being formed that worked for this couple. Each gave a little and they sort of instinctively took turns in being the instigator instead of stand-offs in which one waited for the other. Of course, they had numerous opportunities to practice this method. Most marriages do and one that establishes an unconscious system probably has a better survival rate than one that uses superficial and tentative solutions. Maybe better even than the ones who claim never having any differences. The time period, too, was in their favor. The word "divorce" was not on the tip of every tongue, nor was the idea acceptable, at least not to these salt-of-the-earth people. Mary and Griff knew they would have to make things better between them.

Chapter 16
∂∽∂

Before spring work began, Mary and Griff moved to the Sholes place. The house and barns were not nearly so grand, but the move seemed to give its tenants a new start, even more romantic and ideal with the little family by themselves in their own little cottage. Evan owned the farm and rented it to his son with no special privileges, but none were expected. Griff had reached a new level of maturity and Mary loved him even more. Evan did not seem to resent it and had rented his farm to non-family people with his paying them room and board. This was more business-like and worked for him. Perhaps he was mellowing somewhat as he was in his late seventies.

The little cottage turned out to be a drafty old house. Many winter mornings, there would be frost on the edge of the blankets that were close to the children's mouths. Like any good father and husband, Griff's first chore of the morning was to build good fires in the heating stove and the cook stove. Mary would soon rise and start the oatmeal which was part of their regular breakfast. Then when Griff finished outside chores he came in for bacon and eggs. This was the winter ritual, summer was different. He was doing fine without his dad telling him what to do. The children were growing and Owen would even help look after Sarah. She liked the rubber tire swing that her daddy had put up on a branch of a tree close to the house. Owen enjoyed his red wagon. Both liked the farm animals for their pets. The standard name for any dog was "Old Sport" so their pet sheep was "Old Baa." One day, right after Mary had turned out her freshly baked loaves of bread on the table, "Old Baa" found the screen door ajar and nibbled his way around the table sampling several loaves. Mary was not the calm mother who took everything without exclamation, but she did have reasonable solutions after a little storm of anger. The damaged portions were cut off the loaves and remainders did not go to waste. The children defended their pet and, temporarily at least, helped to keep her out of further trouble.

Griff's pets were a pair of well-trained mules. He had bought them at a farm sale knowing they were a well-regarded team. He paid a good price for them which he justified as a necessary investment. Griff was getting land fever, feeling it was time he bought land of his own, after all he was 28 years old and had a family. He had no intentions of being his father's tenant forever.

News and rumors, quite often very different from each other, were discomforting. News told of a stock market crash in New York. Rumors were saying all business would be affected, and farmers would go broke too. Believing farmers contended that land was always a safe investment and they were proud of their wisdom. How could they know the reverberating effects when the market experts could not avoid the "crash." The Evans lifestyle continued much the same. There were even some exciting new happenings, such as the first "talkie" movie. Mary and Griff accepted the neighbor's offer to keep the children while they went to see Al Jolson in "Sonny Boy." It was an exciting experience and they would certainly want to see the next one that came to town. Who could always be worrying about economic condition of the country? Their '28 Chevrolet was just like new with its deep forest green exterior. The doors shut soundly and the windows rolled up and down with ease.

On a trip to Sioux City to sell cattle, late in the summer, Mary chose a muskrat fur coat and put it on layaway. Griff encouraged her in this purchase. All she had to do was send some money regularly to the store. This could easily be arranged as the egg money was usually considered hers. If the chickens were fed properly and a new batch of young hens added each year, the income was good. By January of 1930, there was one more payment due. Egg prices had gone down along with other farm product prices. Alarm was growing. Mary decided that she was not going to feel right wearing that fur coat amidst the talk that seemed to dominate conversations everywhere. She wrote to the store and they seemed to understand the plight so returned all the money she had paid. With this, she outfitted the whole family, including a fashionable black cloth coat for herself, a suit for Griff, and winter coats for Owen and Sarah. This was all very fortunate as the cash flowed much slower and the value of land went down rapidly. Those winter coats had to serve for an extended period of time. Hard times had arrived.

Early one morning, a neighbor drove into the yard and wanted to talk to Griff only. A neighbor woman who had never mixed with others had come over asking for help. They had just had a shivaree for the couple about a month before. He had been considered a confirmed bachelor, so it surprised many when they were married. The request was for help that Griff had never done. Several men were needed to take the new husband down from the rafters in the barn from which he had hanged himself. Griff needed to talk to Mary about it, but did not want the children to hear, particularly Owen as he was old enough to ask questions. There was much conjecture as to whether he could not adjust to married life or could not handle responsibility in light of the frightening times. It was a disturbing incident to these young adults who were confused about their own affairs.

Chapter 17

Life went on in 1930. There were some barn dances in the spring as the hay lofts were emptied of their crop. These did not require much cash, as the fiddlers donated their time or a collection would be taken to pay them. Maybe the concern of "paying the fiddler" originated from that hard times reality. There were ice cream socials and company dinners on Sunday. Mary and Griff had not attended church regularly since they moved to Sholes. The distance was a factor and they liked being away from Evan's queries. They did miss the involvement of the community, but they were young enough to see it as nosiness instead of caring. The children had been baptized in the home church, but Mary never joined.

In the fall, harvest went on as usual but it lacked enthusiasm. Most of the farmers fed their crops to livestock, but they had no prospects of selling livestock for decent prices. They could eat well themselves, but there was no money to spend on some of the improvements they had become accustomed to. They did have one enthusiastic visitor that fall. Mary's brother Guy came down from the Black Hills of South Dakota.

"I tell you, that is the land of milk and honey," claimed Guy.

"What are you talking about? They can't raise anything up there in those hills," argued Griff.

"Tell us about it," said Mary willing to listen to her brother's good fortune.

"Well, I work in the richest gold mine in the world. I don't get to keep any of the gold, but I get a good day's pay."

"Isn't that awful dangerous? And I don't think you are getting enough sunlight. You're so pale," was big sister's response.

"No, it is not dangerous. They take all kinds of safety precautions. Besides, you get free medical care for the whole family and life insurance if you are killed while working in the mine."

"That doesn't sound very safe if they give you the insurance," debated Griff. "What kind of pay do you get?"

"Most of the jobs pay three dollars a day. Some jobs pay more."

"How do you get down into the mine?" Griff's interest was growing.

"They have guys that let you down in these kind of big open elevators. They go down into the mine through the shaft. That's a good job. They call that a top job."

"What do they wear to work in the mine?" asks practical Mary.

"They wear overalls, a shirt, and a jacket. Have to have a hard hat with a lantern on it. But you know Mary, they clean up in the showers before they come home and a wife doesn't even have to clean up the mess. You do have to pack a lunch, but that would be easier than cooking for threshers."

"How do you go about getting a job like that?" asked the discouraged farmer.

"Well, you go to the employment office and turn your name in, then you go there every day and wait. When there is a job available, you want to be there when they call your name or they go right on to the next name. They call it rustlin'."

"That sounds pretty risky to me. Things will have to get worse here to want to take that chance."

"I wouldn't wait too long. There's lots of people wanting jobs everywhere and the news will get around fast about any place there are jobs."

"Mary and I will have to talk it over."

Only a short time ago, Griff was talking about buying his own farm. Now the thoughts of standing around waiting for a job down under the earth were inwardly terrifying. These were the times of vanquished dreams.

Chapter 18
❧

"I suppose I had better give notice to Dad that we'll be leaving, so he can get a farmer in here by the first of March. Boy, is he going to think I've lost my head."

"No, he'll blame me for leading you on a wild goose chase. But he doesn't have any good advice. There isn't any. And there isn't any hope in staying here either."

"I'm going to loan my mules to Harry Roberts for their keep. He'd like to buy them, but he doesn't have any money."

"Louise said she'd store some of our things for the use of my stove. They just got married and need a stove and they have plenty of storage space in that big house. I know she will take care of it. Sure hate to give it up, even for a little while."

"How much cash do we have between us and starvation?"

"Ninety dollars. But we have a good car and a good supply of clothes and lots of hope for the future to be better." In lean times, Mary could be counted on to supply optimism. Griff needed her now as he never had before.

The 1928 Chevy sedan was packed full with the essentials for whatever was ahead. To Owen and Sarah, ages six and four, it was an exciting adventure. They took turns riding in the front seat with their parents as only one little sitting spot was left in the back. It would take two days to travel the five hundred miles. They would have to stay in a hotel one night, somewhere near Mitchell, South Dakota.

They followed Guy's instructions to his town of Terraville, which seemed to be on a mountain top. The narrow, winding road to get there was treacherous. After warm greetings, they got down to business.

"Have you lined up for a house for us?" asked Mary anxiously.

"Sure have, and it'll cost you just ten dollars a month, furnished," was Guy's enthused reply.

"Well, lead us to it." Griff's was tired and fearful.

"It's just up the hill. I will lead the way."

"Seems like we've done nothing but go uphill since we left home," said Griff, trying to be good natured about dim prospects.

"Actually, you have. This is known as mile high country."

"Where is that mine I'm supposed to work in?"

"Look over there at that hillside," said Guy pointing, "then see that square hole in the side. That's the tunnel to Lead where the mine is. It's only a mile and you walk it. The Homestake Mining Company owns it and uses the train for hauling. It has lights all the way through and all the miners that live here walk it."

To Sarah and Owen this new life was sounding more exciting with each new revelation. Not so to Mary and Griff.

They pulled up to the house. It was painted gray, neat looking but quite small with a narrow front porch. They entered. Mary hurriedly scanned the situation and in her bravest tone of voice said, "This isn't so bad. There is a bright new linoleum rug in the living room and the drop leaf kitchen set has just been painted." Although, Mary was not aware of it, no doubt she had heard her courageous mother take this attitude in one of their many "new homes."

While Griff was wondering how to get some heat in the house, Guy was lighting matches to start small heaters that were almost instant heat. He explained that this was natural gas. It seemed most unnatural to these newcomers from the country. The two bedrooms would be heated sufficiently from the other rooms. The cooking stove operated on gas too. Mary quickly reflected about her nice stove in Nebraska, but thought maybe some of these new ways to do things would be interesting. Besides, no wood had to be carried in and no ashes out. Probably costs a lot.

The Chevy's contents were carried in, Sarah and Owen making their contribution to the adventure, beds were made and they slept their first night in the house where the lights were just shut off, not turned down until the wick went out. Guy arranged to walk with Griff through the tunnel to spend his first day of rustling a job. It consisted of standing and waiting, sitting and waiting, and walking around in the immediate area of the building and waiting. Although a patient man, this was harder on Griff than any day of hard labor. He did this day after day. Owen was placed in school in the first grade, but it became apparent he had not learned much about reading in that previous country school so there was some anxiety about that. The neighbors up the hill were friendly, which was never forgotten. Guy offered to ask his new father-in-law for some pull to get Griff a job. He was a top ladder engineer for the Homestake. Griff's response to the idea was plain.

"I don't want any special favors. If I can't get a job fair and square, I don't want it. After all, I might be working down there with those guys some day and it would be best if we all got the job the same way." Griff's expectations as well as character were showing.

The month's rent was half consumed. The grocery money was disappearing in spite of Mary's frugal cooking. There were ten dollars left of their total cash savings. Griff came rushing home in the middle of the afternoon with the marvelous announcement that he had a job that started the next day. He had to have a hard hat with a lantern on it, miner's boots, and a metal lunch bucket. They drove to Lead that day, three miles by car, to buy the needed objects. That was the end of the ten dollars.

"What are we going to do for groceries until your first paycheck?" realistic Mary asked.

"Now that I'm an employee of the Homestake, we can charge at the Hearst store and they just take it out of the paycheck. And the kids, well all of us, get to go swimming free at the plunge, and Mary you can get books at the library. We get free medical care and they even have a bowling alley in that building where the plunge is," Griff breathlessly revealed this newly-found information.

"Where did you hear all of this? I don't believe it all," countered Mary.

"No, really, they told me at the office when they hired me."

"Well, we're not going to charge all the time. I can see how that would go if we don't watch out. I don't want that paycheck to be gone when you go to pick it up." Wisely, Mary was anticipating the common human failing of abusing the system by too much charging. Although young, their farm background kept them from "counting their chickens before they hatched." They kept their heads and never lost their soul to the company store.

Chapter 19
൙൮

"**S**eems like everyone is friendlier now that I have a job," expressed Griff on a Sunday off, soon after his first paycheck.

"I guess that's natural. Seems people don't want to get acquainted until they know you are going to stay. I feel that way myself," responded Mary.

"We should do something every Sunday like go on a picnic when it's nice enough."

"Aren't you too tired after working all week?"

"Heck no. It's good hard work alright, but it doesn't last late at night like it did on the farm."

"They say there is a lot of beautiful scenery to see in these hills. I'd love to take a ride, and the kids have been wanting to walk through the tunnel."

This started a pattern of Sunday drives and picnics. They never seemed to run out of places to go. There was the lovely Spearfish Canyon Road, the Bear Butte at Sturgis, Rough Rock Falls, the Needles, and the ice cave where they would take the ice cream mix, get ice out of the cave in June or July, crush it and freeze the ice cream. They would sit around on a blanket on the ground and with chattering teeth, eat their treat amidst thick pines and firs. They felt they were having the time of their lives.

While Griff well represented the happy farmer, it seemed he found new happiness working with other men as a team. This job was not so solitary. The men had time to joke and razz each other during lunch or supper depending which shift they worked. When they worked as a team, it would be on a contract to move so much ore in a certain period of time. This was a money-making situation. Griff was soon recognized as a hard worker so was requested on these contract deals. This was probably the most personal respect he had known. He liked getting that from his fellow man. He had made his adjustment from farmer to miner, and he was supporting his family without the help of his father. Self-esteem was high. It was time to buy a house of their own.

Owen was doing better in school now. He had to as little sister Sarah was coming along rapidly with her reading. She had not wanted to go to school because she couldn't read. She was finally persuaded that was supposed to happen at school. Soon, her favorite pastime was to play school after school. Her first grade friends usually wanted her to be the teacher.

"I know the kids are pretty well set in school here in Terraville, but if we buy a house, it should be in Lead. They say the school system is really good over there because the mine pays so much in taxes."

"Yes, and we should take advantage of the recreation over there. I'd even like to bowl."

They started to look at houses for sale. Mary fell in love with one made of shiny varnished, smooth logs which was very popular in this area, but it did prove to be beyond their price range. They settled on a more conservative house that would meet their needs for 800 dollars. Their street was so steep that cars never went up it, only down. The up street was a block over. They built a log garage and soon met their neighbors. One day Mary was outside calling for Sarah Ruth, and the neighbor lady was calling the same name. The two mothers looked at each other and awkwardly approached one another wondering if each already knew her daughter. Finally, they realized each had a Sarah Ruth. They laughed at the coincidence, and friendship came easily with their mutual respect for choice of names.

Children's life-time tendencies show up at a remarkably tender age. Owen revealed his ambitious and congenial traits. He had a paper route of happy customers, who seemed to frequently give him gifts of money. Then when the snow came, he was earning more money scooping snow and keeping some of those same customers happy with his dependability. He was generous with his money as he would buy presents for his mother, mostly. Also, he would spend it freely as he knew there was more where that came from. Sarah early took up womanly ways, not being able to go out and earn money, she tenaciously saved her allowance. She was a contented child, never seeming to tire of her paper dolls, doll house, drawing and coloring, and listening to the radio. She would send for Little Orphan Annie rings and decode the messages. Rarely did she care to have anyone to play with. This worried Mary. The neighbor children would go to the Saturday morning show together and play cowboy and Indian the rest of the day. The admission was 5 cents and they could buy a nickel's worth of candy after the show which would be their supply for the week. One summer they built their club house. They retrieved building supplies from houses that were being torn down. This was a continuous process in Lead, as the mining under the city caused some sinking or unsettling of houses. When a house had to be condemned as unsafe, the mining company would buy the house at a good price and tear it down. The owners were seldom unhappy as this gave them a chance to better their housing. The gang of which Owen was the leader, was very sad the day their club house burned down. A little non-member was lighting matches when the others were in school. Their consolation was the fire brought out the biggest fire engine in town. Their lament was that they did not get to see it.

One of the new family outings by this time was to travel out to the stone covered hill where they were carving the faces of the presidents. Progress seemed slow to the children, but the parents felt they were a part of an exciting time. They would have some of their friends from Nebraska come to visit in the summer. Griff would take them for scary rides around some of the hill roads, they would go for early morning trout fishing expeditions to the clear, rapid running streams, catch a good catch, build a fire and cook breakfast in that beautiful and bountiful natural world. Mary and Griff appreciated their good life, particularly after visiting with their Nebraska friends.

"How are the crops, anyway? You don't seem to be so bad off. At least you get away for a vacation," was Griff's way of sounding them out.

"Well, we wouldn't be here if you hadn't invited us and put us up. Also, there aren't enough crops to keep us busy like there used to be. Besides, it sure feels good to get away from that hot dry weather and seein' those thistles blowing across the fields," responsed their male guest.

"We get a little grain so I keep some chickens. The horses have to have some of that. We get a little corn to feed a few cows and a steer or two so we eat pretty good, but my garden didn't do anything this summer. We just go to the bank to borrow money to put the crop in. If we don't plant anything, we sure aren't going to get any crop. Then we pray and wait for some rain." This was the less protected female version of their plight.

"Does the bank just keep loaning you the money?" Griff asked now that the conversation was opening up.

"Well, I had to take a mortgage out on the farm. If things don't get better pretty soon, the debt will get bad enough, I suppose I could lose the farm. In the mean time, we have a place to live and food to put in our mouths. There isn't any other way that I can see. I just feel sorry for the people who have to be on W.P.A. and stand in line for food."

"We're not the only ones that this is happening to in our age group. Now, some of the older ones like your dad, Griff, are doing OK, as a matter of fact he's loaning money so will end up with more farms. It's the same way it's always been, the rich get richer."

"It's a lot worse down in southern Nebraska. Guess the dust storms are so bad they lose their fences. The weeds and dirt just build up around them."

"It sure hurts to see our men folk go out and plow and plant and not reap."

Mary and Griff were feeling guilty about their new Rockne sitting out in the garage. Studebaker had named their 1932 and 1933 models after the famous Notre Dame football coach, Knute Rockne.

The next summer, their friends who were about ten years older, came for a visit. Their story was not so sad, as they had enough savings to weather the storm of drought and depression. They came for a good time. Prohibition was over, and Deadwood, just three miles from Lead, celebrated "The Days of 76" every summer. They commemorated the lives of Wild Bill Hickock and Calamity Jane by a simulated shoot out on Main Street. The bars were full and there was little concern over a national depression, except a "dance-a-thon" going on in a small dance hall. Unemployed people would enter these to try to win a little subsistence money and food while they were in the contest. They had become a sign of the times.

The visitors wanted to take in all the excitement, but unfortunately, Griff had to work night shift at the particular time. Being the cordial host, they went to see the sights in the day time, but they wanted to take in the night life too.

"Come on Mary, go down to Deadwood with us and show us around," coaxed the company.

"Gee, I've never gone without Griff. You folks just go ahead and go."

"Now you know good natured Griff isn't going to care. I've never seen him mad about anything."

"Well, I have to see if I can get one of the neighbor girls to stay with the kids," said Mary relenting, against her better judgment.

They did the town. They got back to the house about two o'clock in the morning. They had been drinking the popular new "Tom Collins." They were not drunk, just giggly, and it seemed like a good idea to wait up for Griff to come home from work. As he approached the house, he was alarmed about the house being lit up. When he found out the reason, he tried hard not to show his disgruntlement. One doesn't like being reminded of having missed out on a good time because of work. There was a little teasing about that good lookin' guy that asked Mary to dance and Griff faked being really tired and went to bed.

The guests were due to leave the next day after a short night's sleep. Griff cut short his sleeping time also, and cordially sent them off. Almost immediately, he turned to Mary and exploded his harbored anger.

"I never thought I'd see the day that you would do that to me—go out while I'm hard at work, and then flirt around besides. I guess a man can't count on anything."

"I didn't flirt. Ross was just trying to get your goat. And I didn't feel right about going without you. They begged me, but I should have listened to my conscience. I'm sorry."

This readily stated apology came so quickly that Griff hardly knew what to do with the rest of his anger. It subsided and they talked seriously, which they had not done for some time.

"Maybe, we're getting to live kind of like Deadwood, kind of wild. At least it's nothing like we were in Nebraska. I get a little homesick once in a while, but we can't go back yet. We need to go on a trip or something special with the kids. One thing we been doin' right is saving money."

Without being aware, Mary had done what they came to do in settling their differences. They sort of subconsciously took turns in taking the blame or in being in the wrong in the first place. Once blame is assumed, it's difficult to wage a battle. Mary was genuinely contrite, and she momentarily remembered when she was glad for Griff's claiming her and declaring his rights with her. The feeling was still good. The idea of a trip struck a happy note with her, and she instantly thought of going to California. It was the Utopia of the time and the great American family tour. The plans commenced.

Griff could get thirty days off work. Now that was not to be with pay, but nonetheless, a great privilege that came with this job. They would take the time in June and would go through and visit in Nebraska. They would see Griff's dad, of course, his sisters and Mary's sisters. They bought a travel aid that mapped out the way to go. There were no interstates, but there was Highway 30 and Route 66. Griff was so right in this being good for the family. They were renewing family ties and the children were gaining an education in the planning. They wanted to see The Grand Canyon, Salt Lake City, the desert, Boulder Dam, and the ocean. Boulder Dam was nearly finished and was a marvel of the time. This was the summer of 1936. The Rockne was in good condition, however, it had no trunk like most cars of the era. They had a fold up and down rack put on the back. That would hold suitcases and the racks on the fenders would hold odds and ends. They would be staying in motels or cabins. They usually had kitchenettes so the mother in the family didn't get away from cooking on a trip such as this. Owen was excited about things he was going to see and wanted to make sure he had extra spending money to take along. Sarah was thrilled about the new outfits of clothing that were purchased. She would fold and unfold them while planning what combinations she would wear. She liked the sporty white cap that her daddy had. She thought it looked like something she had seen in the movies. She thought her daddy was quite handsome with a hat or cap since he had lost hair from the top of his head some time back. Sarah had always been willing to share her curls with him. This child was like her father—easy going, content. Griff would like to have spoiled her, but she didn't respond to that conditioning. She was more apt to want to wait upon him. Of all the family photos taken on that trip with a Brownie box camera, two were Sarah's favorites. One was Owen, Sarah, and their dad in his white cap standing in the white sand of Carmel by the Sea. The other was she and Owen standing on what appeared to be very close to the edge of a cliff overlooking the Grand Canyon. At age nine, Sarah was developing a romantic attachment to people and places.

Their trip to California was an invigorating family experience. They all grew in knowledge. A greater blessing was the sense of confidence in what their family could do. They certainly were not wealthy, but these children of the great depression were not burdened with the fear that many of their age were. They were made aware of saving by their frugal parents, but they grew up believing that most of what they wanted in life was attainable.

Chapter 20 ᕉᕉ Mary and Griff were feeling good about their parenting, although they would never have voiced it in that way. This was even before Dr. Spock. There was not an abundance of published manuals on how to raise children, but they felt their children were turning out quite well. Sarah was a good student, and Owen was a good Boy Scout earning one badge after another. There was one area of their lives that they knew was not what it should be. "Mary we should be going to church."

"Yes, I know. Which church do you think we should go to?"

"Well, I have asked around and I don't think there is a Congregational like at home. The other church close to home is a Presbyterian. Guess they are quite a bit alike."

"It will take some new clothes. You should get a new suit anyway, and Owen has been complaining about wearing knickers. I can sew dresses for Sarah and me."

Owen's new suit came with two pair of trousers, one long pants and the other knee length so he did not get his way completely. Sarah's Sunday best was a soft, silky rayon with the new elastic dirndl waistline. Although, she liked to wear coveralls for play, she loved to dress up.

Mary and Griff went to church, while Owen and Sarah went to Sunday School. Sarah came skipping out of the building to meet her parents, elated that she knew some of the other kids from her class at school. Marshall Hunkins was one of the boys that she thought was nice. He knew the answers to lots of questions. She had early in life come to respect this ability.

"Hunkins, that's the name of the superintendent of schools," Mary quickly summed up.

"Yeh, and I think I saw Biorge there too. You know he's the general manager of the mine. I don't know for sure. I've only seen him a time or two," Griff added.

"Did anyone speak to you at Church?"

"They spoke, but I didn't know a soul. Sure didn't feel like going to church at home."

"Well, we can't decide on one Sunday, but they sure did seem high toned. Probably too rich for our blood."

Sarah in her quiet way, often overheard conversations. This one was strange to her as she had never heard her parents talk about this sort of thing. High toned was not meaningful to her but "too rich" was clear, however, she thought her family was rich.

"Mommy, who is richer than we are?" she asked looking up from her book.

"Oh my, there are lots of people richer than we are," Mary easily stated now that she had been strengthened by her happy child's faith in their status. She hoped secretly that life would never change that blithe spirit.

They went to church a few more Sundays, and then sent the children to Sunday School. Of course, they went to the Christmas Eve program. They did not discuss it, but Mary and Griff knew this was a negative in their lives. They did not know the solution. Time would have to reveal that to them.

Chapter 21
೭⊷৯

Owen and Sarah came rushing home and burst into the house arguing which one got to tell the news. Owen won.

"We're going to be on stage down at the theater. Our whole dance class. Mom, you have to go to our next lesson to talk to the teacher because we're going to have costumes and everything. Gene and I are going to have our faces black and wear straw hats. Boy, is that going to be fun!"

"Me too, Mom. I'm going to wear a red suit like a swim suit with a big black bow on it and a whole bunch of us are going to dance in a line. I already know most of my steps, see."

This was going to be exciting. Mary was glad that they both were more enthused about their dance lessons than they were about piano lessons. It had become the challenge of every day to get practice time in. Owen would get up early in the morning to practice. That was not appreciated, but certainly he was not to be discouraged. Sarah became an expert procrastinator and often bedtime came, and she had not practiced. If there was a chance of going to the movie on Friday night, she made a point of getting busy right after school. This was a grievance to Mary and Griff now that the piano was completely paid for. Mary often recalled how Sarah had overheard their conversation about making the last payment and promptly relayed it to the neighbors who appreciated knowing. She then came home and reported proudly what she had done. Her childlike oblivion to duplicity caused some discomfort to her parents, but they did not want to teach her to be any other way.

The children did well in the dance recital. Owen seemed to do these activities without anxiety, but Sarah did get very nervous. She would twist her hair, blink her eyes, pull at her clothes but perform with ease seeming to enjoy being on stage. There was the time in first grade, when the elastic cord on her face mask broke just before the group was to go on stage. She refused to go, staying behind the curtain crying, mostly because her mother had worked hard to make her costume that essentially was never used. Mary, of course, had some bad moments sitting in the audience wondering where her child was. As soon as possible, she went backstage to find the very unhappy Sarah.

Because Sarah was usually so remorseful when things went wrong, she seldom heard harsh scolding from either parent. They would try to console her instead. The dance show didn't have any of that pain, so they felt Sarah was outgrowing her shyness.

And so the days of ordinary families fly by. The concerns are confronted and the joys are absorbed as a group giving meaning to the word family. Each experience binds the tie and patterns the way that the children meet life. Mary and Griff were doing their best and they never questioned whether their lives were meaningful. They did not require that additional ego fulfillment to a life style that was natural and good.

Chapter 22
༄·৩

"**M**om, I can hardly reach around you. How come you are getting so fat?" Sarah inquired as she hugged her mother while leaning against the upright gas heater on a cold January evening.

"Yeh, I noticed that, too, and I bet I know why," chimed in a much older and wiser Owen.

Mary darted a look to Griff and he nodded, meaning "we better tell them the news."

"Well, you see, you're going to have a new brother or sister. That's what I'm carrying around in my body. The baby will be born in April so we will be a bigger family. Won't that be nice?"

"That's just what I thought. It better be a boy and it better not cry all the time."

Sarah, not so worldly wise, was overwhelmed. She sensed that she shouldn't ask too many questions, but could not figure out how the baby would get out of there.

"I want a sister to play dollhouse with me, and I'll help take care of her too."

The battle waged until birth. Owen thought the clothes they were getting ready for the baby looked awful girlish. Sarah put a month's wear on them patting and folding the soft, pretty garments.

In the meantime, plans were being made to honor Evan Evans on his eighty-fifth birthday in Nebraska about the middle of April. Griff's sisters were planning it and they wanted all the grandchildren there. This was very inconvenient because of the baby that was due about that time. Mary should not go. If the other children were going to miss school, Owen and Sarah could too. Sarah knew that she had to complete a certain number of pages for the Palmer Method of handwriting, which had to be sent in on a certain deadline. If any student did not make this date, he or she would receive an "F" on his or her report card. Sarah finished everything except the letter to Mr. Palmer. Her teacher assured her she could finish that in the one day she had after getting back from her grandfather's birthday. Owen lined up a substitute to deliver his papers, and failed to see that leaving was such a difficult process.

Sarah did not like going without her mother, and she didn't really like her yellow knit skirt and top that her mother had knit while taking lessons. She liked the color, but the skirt was too tight. She was one of the younger cousins, and didn't know what the older girls were talking about all the time. Her grandpa hardly talked to them. He just handed out peppermint candies with black fuzz on them from his suit pocket. He could hear better when her dad talked to him in some funny sounding words. Griff had retained some Welsh language, which his dad seemed to understand. He had always insisted that his family speak American in America, but now he seemed to respond best to the old language. Sarah was anxious to get back home.

Her mother was alright, but the baby had not yet arrived. Now Sarah must go to school and finish that letter for penmanship class. She had developed into a conscientious student, and though studies came easy for her, she was a worrier until she finished her assignments. The one remaining class period proved to be insufficient time as she kept making some error part way through the letter. The teacher calmly announced that this was the day that all work was to be finished, and Sarah panicked. She could not even explain her problem. This was a new experience. She did not know how to ask for special consideration. She would get an "F" on her report card. She did not cry at school, but as soon as she was off the school ground she ran and cried all the way home. Mary was alarmed at her child's concern but was practically immobile with the imminent baby's birth. Griff was due home from work any minute. He could go talk to Sarah's teacher. That wasn't his talent, but he went. Sarah's dad was her savior. A deal was struck, and she would receive a "C." She remembered that as the worst crisis of her whole childhood.

A few days later, Sarah and Owen were rushed off to school, a nurse was there and Dad was not going to work. When they came home for lunch, there was a baby brother sleeping in the bassinet that had awaited him. Owen reminded Sarah that he had won with a brother, but Sarah never expressed a single regret and instantly loved that brother who was eleven years younger.

   Mary could have delivered the baby at the hospital with full employee benefits. She held her sentimental notion that her other children were born in a home, not a hospital, and that was fine for this one too. He was named David. It seemed the household was never really calm again. He was a fussy baby, and when he outgrew that, he was so cute with his big blue eyes and blonde curly hair that his every antic was laughed at and enjoyed.

Chapter 23
ᗕᗝᗕᗝ

One of the popular enticements of this time was "Banknite." This was held one night a week at the theater to encourage attendance to the movies. Of course, people had found out how to get around it by simply being on the premises when the winning name was called, which had been registered prior to the drawing. The amount was up to two hundred dollars. Mary and Griff had taken their place outside the theater just moments before the name "Mary Evans" was called. She collected the money in cash. Excitement found new meaning. This money would have to be spent on something special. Their choice of a new car was the same as Claudette Colbert's or so the advertisement said, which was a stratosphere blue Dodge. It took Mary's winnings and about six hundred dollars more. Griff always said, smiling, "I knew that Banknite was going to cost me in the end."

That was the same year that they bought their first refrigerator. Mary always seemed to have remodeling projects in mind and Griff was cooperative in carrying them out. One interesting plan was the arch made between the living and dining rooms. Then they transformed the attic to a room for the boys and Sarah had her own room downstairs. They took out the stairway to gain more room and put in a pull down ladder type stair that closed up in the ceiling when not in use. It was the first thing to show to company and they did have lots of company. They learned to play Bridge and Pinochle, and would entertain those groups. There were friends from Griff's job and Mary's bowling team. There were neighbors from Terraville and Lead neighbors who had moved, but they never seemed to lose track of anyone. One of Mary's sisters of the older three had moved to Lead in the worst part of the depression and had also benefited by a job with "The Homestake" mining company. She and her husband had four daughters, and with Mary's brother there she felt good about having that much family around. Mary never abandoned her position as eldest daughter. The maternal aunt who had taken her six-month-old baby sister and raised as her own now needed an anchor in her life. Her children were grown and married and her husband left her. There had been trouble before. Baby Ruth grew up feeling she might have been to blame. She also had very little faith in the staying quality of men. Mary persuaded her aunt to come to Lead and stay with them until she could find something to do. They found an elderly widower who needed a housekeeper in a very fine house. Her aunt responded best to other's needs and the plan worked fine for several years until the old gentleman died and she reunited with her husband. Separation seemed to be a plausible solution to marital problems at that time.

The year of 1939 was marked as having two world fairs — New York and San Francisco. The latter was not officially a world fair, but it had more lure to the Evans family. They could combine it with a visit to Yakima, Washington, where Mary's next younger sister and family had settled as a result of the drought and depression. The Dodge was new and the baby old enough to go. Once again, it was a great experience for Owen and Sarah, but not so for little brother David. He became seriously dehydrated after joining the big folks in the delight of eating bing cherries fresh from the tree, then following it with his regular milk supply. The doctor knew the danger, but it was not commonly known. All concerned felt so bad about endangering the little fellow's life. Sarah became a regular "mother hen." Even though she had lost her position as baby of the family, she never showed any signs of sibling rivalry.

Of all the sights they saw at the fair, the one Sarah remembered most was seeing, under a microscope, the Lord's Prayer printed on the head of a pin. There was also a little spat between her mom and dad which she did not understand at the time. Her dad wanted to see some show, and her mother said, "What are the kids and I supposed to do while you watch that show?"

He mumbled something about being his only chance to see Sally Rand. That must have been his most selfish moment. He did not go to the show.

They returned home and life seemed lacking in high points. Sarah and Owen quarreled more over doing the dishes and minding David. It no doubt was a letdown after the big trip. Griff had a bad cold and the cough lingered on, concerning him enough to go to the doctor. There was some conjecture about miners getting dust in their lungs. Griff might fall into this category and it was recommended that he not continue working in the mine too long. Difficult decisions were forthcoming.

Chapter 24
తోపడ్

Sometimes life's questions are answered by a natural turn of events. The mining, even though far below their home, was causing some changes and the condemning process was under way for their home and several others. This did not cause alarm as they knew the procedure. However, it would require a decision on a new place to live. The settlement with the Homestake would be fair and they were somewhat pleased at the prospects of a new house. But, maybe this was a message about Griff's health. And then, a telegram arrived. Evan Evans, Griff's father had died. The family would go to the funeral. He was the only grandparent the children had known.

"What's a funeral, Mom?" asked Owen in his usual curious style.

"It's a way we show respect for the dead, and Christians believe in praying before the body is buried," Mary answered as simply as possible remembering her children had not been to a funeral.

"Will Grandpa go to Heaven?" asked Sarah.

"We believe he will. This is our Christian belief," Mary responded thinking these questions were getting harder to answer.

Owen, anxious to get on to a different subject wondered how many more miles.

"We are going to make the whole trip in one day, so you might as well sleep a while, or at least, don't ask that question for a while. We sure have it a lot better than when we made our first trip to South Dakota eight years ago," Griff remembered vividly.

"You kids were better travelers then and you hardly had space to sit," Mary chimed in.

The kids became interested in road signs and Mary and Griff conjectured about their past and immediate future.

"Do you think your dad left anything to you in his will?"

"I don't look for too much, but he didn't seem angry with me at the time of his birthday. He did say he had three farms, so it would be reasonable to divide it up evenly with we three remaining heirs."

"Would you go back to farming if he wills you a farm?"

"Well, it would be the answer to the question of miner's consumption. I would just as soon never find out if I'm getting it. Would you go back to being a farmer's wife again?"

"Yes, I think that's where you belong, and I have had an easy life for eight years, but I like the idea of going home."

Griff liked hearing Mary say that. This conversation had stirred interest in the reading of the will. After proper respects were shown, and not with a sense of greed but rather with a desire of what life had mapped out for them, the will was read. Griff had figured his dad right. He was to receive the last farm they had lived on which was fair, since he had asked for that eleven years ago. This meant the home place would go to younger of the two sisters. She made a proposition to Griff.

"Griffith, you are the only boy and I think you should have the home place."

"That's nice you feel that way, but if Dad wanted it this way, maybe we should leave it alone."

"Well, there's more to the story. We couldn't afford to start up farming. We've been lucky to keep food on the table these last years. You've been doing better. Besides, I'm afraid we'd lose the farm after while, and I've been hard enough on the Evans name already. Dad would turn over in his grave if we lost a farm. So I'll trade you deals, then you can pay me the difference in the valuation of the farms, and we can use that to start farming."

Mary and Griff had to analyze their situation. They had savings and they would be getting a settlement on their house, but it might cramp their style a little. However, herein lies the answers to all those questions that were pending. The idea of an Evans farming the Evans place had appeal. Griff's pride was touched. He took his sister's offer, and made plans to be ready to start on the first of March, 1940. The depression was over, probably because of war in Europe, or because President Roosevelt had led his people away from the fear that had tumulted a worldwide economy to despair. The drought, too, seemed to be over. Blessings were falling upon these salt of the earth people.

Chapter 25
📖

Adults generally think that children make adjustments easily to family moves. Most any parent, however, who experienced that as a child, is more sensitive to the issue and treats it with concern. Mary and Griff wanted this transition to be pleasant for their children. David, of course, was too young to be affected. Sarah had become overly conscientious about her school work and was a fretter. She was not an unhappy child, but was not gregarious with her peers. She was obedient to her parents and very helpful and caring with her little brother. Owen seemed to adapt to whatever situation he was in, even though he was not as good a student as Sarah. His teachers always reported that he would get along in life just fine. Boy Scouts was important to him, but again, he was adaptable.

"I can finish all my badges for my Eagle Scout award, but I can't get it before we move. The Court of Honor isn't going to be until March," reported Owen after a Scout meeting.

"Oh, that's too bad. Are you going to feel bad about that? You know how we talked about moving after the end of the first semester in January," responded Mary beginning to feel there wasn't going to be a perfect time to make the move.

"Oh, they can just send it to me. I didn't work for it just to stand up in front of a bunch of people. I want to get moving 'cause I want to learn to drive a tractor."

Owen had picked up on that excitement among the farm boys on the last two trips to Nebraska. The boys even argued which make of tractor was the best. No doubt they were imitating their fathers, since tractor farming was just getting a foothold as a way of life, and since times were just a little better.

Mary appreciated his attitude especially because Sarah had been comforted somewhat by the semester end decision. She was afraid of the county exams that eighth graders had to take in the spring. She had heard they had to pass geography and agriculture of Nebraska, none of which she had studied. This was the same little girl who didn't want to go to school without knowing how to read. Owen would go right into high school without that concern. By going in January, they would live in town for two months and they would pay tuition for Sarah to finish the semester in town where they did not have to take county exams. This child could not feel that her parents were not considerate of her fears.

Shortly before moving day, Sarah came home from school with a small gift box.

"See what my class gave me today. It's a Black Hills gold necklace. They said it would help me remember them. I didn't know they even cared I was leaving." This always congenial child was slowly realizing that her peers liked her and she had never particularly strived for that or worried about it. There had been their little dance group of four boys and four girls. Owen was in this group, and one of his friends was supposed to be Sarah's partner and one of her friends was Owen's partner. They had records to play and each of the girls could play one or two popular tunes on the piano that provided their music. They brought ideas they had about dancing to their practice times in the various homes, because none had any lessons. This was all in preparation for the big school dance, which also was held before they were to move. Although, Sarah always had a secret crush on some boy, she rarely got to know them. She continued to like any boy she liked in the first place. This dance partner was not one of those. Owen and his partner seemed to be in love and she envied them. Their favorite song was "I'll Never Smile Again," and Sarah felt so bad for them to have to part. All of this at age twelve. Romantics, too, must be born.

There were dinners and parties for their folks, too. Owen and Sarah were not the only ones who were going to be missed.

Mary and Griff were methodically planning their move so they could save every dollar they could for their new undertaking. Griff bought a used, but sound truck, to do their own moving. He'd drive the truck and Mary the car. It would take two days with this arrangement, and they had a house rented in town so had a home as a destination. Two months later, they would move to the farm. In the meantime he would move his sister's family to their farm and save them money as well. The truck would come in handy for hauling equipment purchased at the farm sales that he planned to attend to complete his readiness for farming. Griff was amazed at himself in the way he adjusted to his old manner of making a living, especially when he had been so content being a miner. He felt he was meant to be a farmer. It took more headwork and planning to live without a regular income. It took patience to put seed into the ground and wait until it grew. And it took faith. Griff seemed to be blessed with these qualities plus a good woman as a helpmate.

Chapter 26
෬ೲ෧

The new decade of the 40s marked a new beginning for the Evans family, as well as significant change in the lives of every citizen of the United States. It even had its own sound.

The 40s were not a centennial of any specific historical event, nor did they have bicentennial connections. The U.S.A. did not exist in 1740. So this new decade carried high expectations to be original and different. The cost of originality was high. War was declared when the decade was still new and the first half was consumed by that world struggle, the last half, dedicated to adjustment to change. The lives of ordinary people such as the Evans family served to mirror these vast ramifications.

The first year and eleven months before war were particularly important in the lives of Owen and Sarah. Owen fit right in and was accepted by the farm boys in spite of his refusal to wear overalls to school. He insisted on wearing his pleated trousers with a gold chain draped on one side. This was the midwest modification of the "Zoot Suit." The other boys wore clean striped bib overalls with fresh starched collar shirts. Because the Evans had moved from the city, it was OK to be different. Besides, Owen was short but fast and alert on the basketball court. He also had that boyish charm that had won over his teachers since third grade. He did experience some proving himself, pugilistically. Perhaps, it was because he had training in boxing while still in Lead, so he was quick to put up his "dukes." Or it might have been the "new kid on the block" syndrome. It happened mostly in neighboring towns when he was there for some competition or special event. His school friends tended to support him or embroil him in the first place. When he came home with blood on his white band uniform, he had to deal with his mother. There was nothing "sissy" about Owen, the greatest of commendations for young men of that time.

Sarah experienced a transformation in personality, which she later ascribed to seemingly insignificant events. Very soon after moving to their temporary home in town, Mary sent Sarah to the local store down the street. As she carried out her errand with very few words exchanged because of her shyness, the store owner said, "I'll bet you're Mary and Griff's girl, aren't you." Her positive answer did not reveal all that this did for her. It was as if she had been claimed by her homeland. A very similar feeling was fostered at the Congregational Church which they, as a family, attended immediately after their move. Sarah had a little difficulty understanding the imperativeness of this after not going for so long in Lead. And then she grew in understanding. After the service, the people gathered in the back part of sanctuary and greeted one another and the Evanses on their coming home. This turned out to be more handshaking and warmhearted greeting than Sarah had ever seen. Her parents sure did seem happy. She remembered how sad her parents were that time they went to church and no one spoke to them. No wonder. She couldn't think of any time that she felt so good with this many people around. Before they left the premises that bright January morning, they had been invited to dinner next Sunday, Sarah and Owen were asked to join the confirmation class which would join the Church in the spring, Mary was urged to come to Ladies' Aid, and Griff was reminded that he was most welcome filling his father's shoes. Quiet, unassuming Sarah was released. She did not become rowdy, rebellious, or bold. The change came more in the form of inner confidence. She did not fret so much about her studies and found that she did just as well. Her nervous habits of hair twisting and blinking seemed to just disappear. Other kids asked her questions and seemed interested in her answers. It was fun to go to school each day for social reasons. The boys she liked seemed to like her back, especially one. She had seen him first that day they had taken some things out to the farm. He was the youngest son of the family that had lived there with Grandpa all those years. She thought he treated her as if he were much older, but anyhow he was nice. Then that day at church their eyes met. A time or two he had brought something for the teacher from upstairs where the principal's office and the high school were, and he winked at her from the door. She would quickly look away and wonder who else saw his attention to her but eagerly wait for the next similar happening.

Sarah liked her teacher, too. Both seventh and eighth grades were in that one room, but the teacher seemed to know each of them well and was warm and friendly to Sarah. She recognized Sarah's quickness in learning and appreciated it as it was a full load to teach all subjects to two classes. Also there was a retarded boy in Sarah's class. She was a little afraid of him, but always talked to him kindly. After those years that Sarah never really cared whether she was alone or not, she found every occasion for being with others a source of happiness. This new life was so good. She must remember to say her prayers to thank God.

Still much more happened in those months before the war to shape the minds and souls of those young people. Griff had spent his youth in that same community with many of the same influences, and did not see many differences. The business of earning a living usually demands so much attention from the parent generation, that they are rarely good evaluators of the times. Most of the kids were supposed to be doing their share of work, and as long as that got done and they didn't get into deep trouble, the parents felt they were doing fine. "Don't borrow or go looking for trouble," was a popular philosophy of that time.

"Well, Sarah, your money grew today," was Griff's seemingly calm report not too many weeks after they had moved to the country and officially started farming.

"Oh Dad, I'll bet you mean I have some new baby pigs." It didn't take much guessing since she had been waiting for the news since she had invested her 12 dollars in a pig due to have little ones anytime.

"You're no fun to try to surprise, but you don't know how many." Griff enjoyed this pleasant taunting of his daughter.

"How many? How many?"

"You have eleven healthy little pigs. There were two more but they didn't live. That is a very big litter, and you can't expect all of them to live. And you might not raise all of them either. A farmer learns that he can't count chickens before they hatch, so don't start counting your money yet." He knew Sarah was a saver and a planner.

"Did Owen's mother pig have her babies?" Sarah was thinking she might be ahead of her brother for once.

"Yes, my sow had seven pigs early this morning. I don't see why you have to talk that baby talk. Nobody says "mother pig." You will just have to help come out and feed all those pigs of yours." Owen was showing a little sibling rivalry.

"Now Owen, Sarah won't be out in the barn helpin' with the pigs. Evans women don't work in fields and they don't work in the barns. And they don't talk like men either, so don't be making fun of your sister's talk. They take care of the chickens and the house. You feed her pigs while she irons your shirts and I don't want any keepin' track either." Griff surprised himself with the authority he showed in this explanation of what was to be. He couldn't have made that up about the Evans women; he must have heard his dad say that even before his mother died. Anyway, he was glad he said it.

"Do I get to buy a car with my pig money, Dad?" Owen asked, quickly accepting his dad's proclamation.

"Well you kids do have to have a car to go to school those four miles every day or would you rather ride a horse?"

"Ride a horse!" both exploded simultaneously.

"I don't even know how to get on one," Sarah admitted.

"What would you do with one after you got there?" Owen questioned realistically.

"Oh, that isn't such a big problem; there are barns in town. Of course you have to pay for it, maybe a car and gasoline would be just as saving since I'd have to buy riding horses. Guess a car wouldn't be a bad idea."

"Boy, I know just the car for me — a '35 Ford!"

"My gosh, our family car is a '38. You're thinking a little too fancy for your britches," commented his father, wondering where this boy got his ideas.

"Where do I fit in this picture? I am going to have some money too, but I'm not old enough to drive, so maybe I don't want to spend it on a car," added Sarah.

"Well, let's see, I think I won't charge either one of you for feeding the pigs, and you split the price of a car that will get you to school on these roads. After all, we do have two miles of gravel, but it's those other two that are not graveled that we have to worry about. I've seen it so muddy it took horses to pull out a Model T."

"What kind of car do you think, Dad?" Owen returned quickly to the car conversation.

"They say '30 or '31 Model A's are good in the mud and easy to overhaul if the engine goes bad."

"Why do I have to help pay for it when I can't drive it?" says Sarah guarding her savings that do not yet exist.

"Because it's the way you are going to get to school, that's why," answered Dad firmly.

"Why do you have to be such a tightwad? Gee whiz, we just get something goin' and you have to worry about your money." Owen had recognized this trait in his sister early on.

"Owen and I will be scouting around at the sales and seein' what we can find."

"Well, if I have to help pay for it, it better be nice inside, nice seats and stuff."

So much of what these children learned was based on common sense. Mary and Griff knew no other way to approach anything.

The family Dodge served to get them to school until the Model A was located. It needed an overhaul and new interior. Uncle Bill had been a mechanic in Omaha, and they would get him to do the job before spring field work started. Owen was not afraid to try the re-upholstering project. He and Sarah bought the material with Mary's promise to sew where needed to fit the seats. They could be removed to facilitate matters. The new material was placed in the top inside and on the doors. Owen was just as particular as Sarah in wanting their car to be nice. They were more united than they ever let on.

Now Griff could turn to the matter of his new tractor. He listened to Owen's input. "From what I hear, Dad, most of the guys think the Farmall is best. I guess it has more power. That's what we want, especially when we start plowing." Griff was pleased with his son's interest.

"Speaking of plowing, Owen, I want you to walk out west of the cow barn with me. Something I want you to know."

"Sure Dad, I want to know everything about this farm."

They walked a short distance to a triangular shaped, three acre area with a lone tree on the vertex of the angle. There was just a hint of green coming through a sort of thatched grass.

"That piece of land has never been plowed, not ever, not since the beginning of time. I don't ever want it to be. That's kind of a promise I made to myself, but I want your help and when David is old enough, if I'm not around, you see to it that he understands. They call it prairie hay, you can cut it and stack it, but don't plow the ground."

"Gee Dad, that's neat. I sure wouldn't want to change that." If Owen ever needed to get in touch with God or himself, he'd walk out there and look at that piece of earth that man had not changed.

Father and son were in tune. A Farmall H tractor was purchased. Seeing his tractor with its bright red finish and big black rubber tires sitting out in front of the big gray hay barn, his older son sitting in the driver's seat and the little one standing behind, Griff realized his once vanquished dream had been renewed. He was a land owner and a tiller of the soil.

That May, Sarah graduated from the eighth grade with a very good average, even with taking the county exams. They did not have to pass them, but the teacher wanted to compare her students with the country schools as she was quite confident they would do well, and they did. The town kids put on a banquet for the graduates from the surrounding schools, so they would know one another when they went to high school. Sarah liked these new kids and started looking forward to being in high school. Three of them were from west of town and it was later arranged that they would ride to school with her and Owen. Each would pay a dollar a week. Sarah liked the idea that her money was making money. It went into a "Kitty" for repairs. When the other kids crawled into the car with muddy boots at their arranged pick up spot, Sarah was sorry for their bargain.

The weather was a greater test to her parents. The early summer breezes were gently wafting the headed out shafts of the small grain fields. A bountiful harvest was the expectation of this first season of returning to the farm. The gentle breezes changed to fierce, and ominous dark clouds gathered.

"Looks like hail," was the somber analysis from Griff. The farmer ability of reading the skies had not left Griff. He was correct. Hail destroyed that waving grain and planted some fears in its place.

Griff's sister and family soon drove into the farmyard and got out of the car with long dismal faces. Though some distance away, their crop had been destroyed too. They knew where they would find empathy — family in a similar situation.

The sidewalk that led to the kitchen door, not the front door was slippery from melting hail, but the grass in the yard was still covered white.

Mary came bursting out the door, completely in command of the situation, "You kids take these dishpans and scrape up the hail. I'm going to whip up a batch of ice cream and we'll all help freeze it. This time we won't have to go to town to buy a block of ice. Sarah, go up to the wash house and get the freezer and the salt."

Mary's resourcefulness served as the comic relief in this tragedy. The other actors dutifully performed. Soon the handle of the freezer would turn no more even with man's strength, indicating the ice cream was frozen. Next, Griff pulled his pliers out of that certain pocket of his overall, applied them to the paddle of the freezer and proved the wonder of hail and salt doing its job. Mary passed out the dishes as everyone lined up to get them filled by Griff.

"You put in just the right amount of cream, Mary."

"Oooh, this is cold."

"Yeah, it makes my head ache."

"Oh, you sissy, just eat it and quit complaining."

"It's so good, but it makes me shiver."

"We sure put that hail to good use, didn't we?" Enough time had elapsed that the adults could now deal with the problem.

"They had a pretty good small grain crop around here last year, I heard, so we can buy enough to feed the horses, pigs, and chickens this year and hope for better next year. I guess we knew what we were getting into in this business." Griff was thinking out loud.

What better prayer for accepting God's will could have been uttered?

Later that summer Owen and Sarah found out what fun was all about. "Do we get to go to town Wednesday night, Mom? Have they called on the party line yet to say what the movie will be?"

"Is the cream can about full, Sarah? I suppose we'll have to take it to town, if it is," glad that her children were happy and anticipating one day after another. "How is the egg case?

Is it getting full, too? That's sort of your department. Are you keeping plenty of straw in the nests so the eggs stay clean?"

"Don't worry Mom. I can't stand dirty eggs. The men need to keep plenty of straw on the floor too." Sarah was learning to carry out her responsibilities.

"What's so much fun about going to town every Wednesday and Saturday night, anyway?"

"The kids are a lot of fun at the free movie. The boys tease us girls which is OK, if they don't get too rough. Mostly, they just throw popcorn in our hair. That boy that used to live here with Grandpa is always nice. He buys me a candy bar. Then on Saturday night, it's good to hear the band play in the park. I'd like to play in the band when I get in high school. Owen said he'd like to, too."

Mary was enjoying getting a little more information than usual, when Griff came into the house to give directions as to where the forthcoming truck should let out its load. When he noticed Sarah standing there listening, he referred to the "gentleman cow" that was arriving. With that kind of protected childhood, Sarah felt a lifetime obligation to maintain a genteel language. What a gentle way to guide a child.

Owen and Sarah went to confirmation classes on Sunday evening and later Christian Youth Group. It was early understood that they would not go to dances on Sunday night. It was never a fought-about issue as they were given enough choices of other sorts. Occasionally, there would be a dance down at the town gym at the end of Main. It had been a sale barn until recently when a new gym floor, standard basketball court, was put in along with a stage. It was used for all important events. In the winter, it was heated by two huge pot bellied stoves that warmed sufficiently when the iron bellies were a glowing red.

It became known that Sarah could and would teach anyone to dance who wanted to learn. "You just take two steps one way and one back. After you get that, you just turn different ways and add your own ideas. Just keep the beat. It's real easy. Now let's try."

Many of her students turned out to be good dancers with their own style. That step could even be worked into the jitterbug with a little imagination. They learned new steps by watching the movies and then trying them out. There was not a

young person in the vicinity who ever had a formal dance lesson, but they were not afraid of failure so experimented and
succeeded.

There was only one boy that Sarah could not entice onto
the dance floor, and probably the one she most wanted to. The
one who bought her candy bars. This was the source of one of
the worst events of her young life. Mary's sister and brother-in-
law from Lead were visiting in Nebraska to attend a family
funeral. School was in session so their four girls were not along.
Sarah had overheard some conversation about how strict they
were with their girls, because they might just want to go to the
library to see boys, and they didn't want their girls to get wild.
Sarah, with missionary zeal, persuaded her aunt and uncle and
parents to come down and watch them dance after they had
finished grocery shopping and visiting. She kind of wanted
them to see boys and girls having a good time without doing
anything bad, although Sarah did not really know what was
bad. Well, her favorite boy friend did not want to pay admission since he had no intention of dancing, so he signaled Sarah
to the door to just come out and sit in his car with him. He was
a fine young man which was a good thing since Sarah was
weakened in his presence. She went with him. The adults came
to watch the young people dance but there was no Sarah. They
left soon and Sarah returned.

"Your folks and some other people were here looking for
you, Sarah."

"Where were you? Bet I know where. Boy, are you going
to be in trouble."

"Why did you ever do that dumb stunt, Sis? Boy, I didn't
like the look on Mom's face."

Sarah had never been more uncomfortable. She'd never
been in trouble with her folks before, and now her aunt and
uncle would know about it, too. "Oh, what a terrible mistake I
made, but I didn't really do anything wrong." She had to wait
until the end of the dance to go home with Owen, because that
was how it had been arranged. When they got home, both had
to let their parents know they were home and what time it was.
That part was normal, but Sarah slept very little that night
worrying what morning would bring. It was as bad as she had
feared.

"Where were you when we stopped at the dance, last night?"

"I went out to talk to Paul."

"Why couldn't you talk to him inside the dance hall?"

"Because he didn't want to come in."

"If you always do what he wants to do, you'll end up in trouble."

"Oh, they were just doing a little necking—no harm in that." Surprisingly, Owen was defending his sister, but she didn't know if that word necking was helping her cause or not.

"Well, nice girls don't leave dances to go sit in cars, so we just won't have anymore of that! Hereafter, you'll not accept a date or go out with any boy until you are 16."

At age 14, that sounded like a whole lifetime away, but she did not whine or plead her cause. She did not blame Paul and hoped he would stay interested since he was the love of her life. At least, she wasn't banned from seeing him at school. She would tell him about it Monday.

"It's my fault that you're in trouble with your folks. Darn, I just wanted to talk to you for a little awhile and get you away from all those other boys that you are teaching to dance." Paul came through in heroic fashion and Sarah loved him more.

"It would help if you learned to dance."

"I promise I'll learn, but I thought it would be better if I learned from someone other than you."

Sarah wasn't sure she understood that, but she knew she did not feel romantic about any of the boys she did teach.

Several months later, the test came. The end of the basketball season prompted the boys who had gone out for the sport, which meant most of the boys in high school, to plan a roller skating party. They would have to have dates. A group plan usually helps, remarkably so, to expedite Mother Nature's urging. Owen was the first to announce it in the Evans household.

"Why don't you just ask your sister for your date, and that would keep everything simple,"Mary suggested.

While Owen was scowling at the suggestion, Sarah voiced her objection, "No, thank you. If I can't get my own date, I don't want to go! Can I go if someone asks me?" remembering the ruling of the distant past.

This was going to call for some discussion between Mary and Griff. They were learning how to parent teenagers before it was such a widely-discussed subject. Mary would assume leadership and Griff support.

"Well, we'll see. Just be sure you get our permission before you accept any date." The interpretation had loosened a little and Sarah was brightening.

"I already asked Sue, and she said she would like to go and she didn't have to ask at home first. Of course, she is older," said Owen wanting to keep his sister in place, but not wanting to hurt her too much.

"Oh, you mean Ruby and Tom's Sue? That's good, I'm sure they will have rules about when she has to get home and so forth."

The next day at school was proof of Paul's heroism. It all happened picking up the ping pong paddles, deciding whose turn it was to play, and he said, "Will you ask your parents if you can go to the roller skating party with me?"

Later, she thought about how he did not ask her if she wanted to. Guess he knew how she felt. This must have been the beginning of her unbeguiling way with men. She reported verbatim to her parents and permission was granted with a few reminders.

They had a glorious time and several of those first date situations turned into lasting relationships. They were not just fickle children and they were imitating their parents in choosing partners they really cared about.

These events and others developed a zest for life in these young people's hearts, a desire to make it meaningful, and a love for country that endowed them with strength to see them through the war-torn years that ensued.

Chapter 27
❧❧❧

It was an early December Sunday and four families were gathering in the large country dining room of the Evans' farmstead. Each family brought something, but the hostess fixed the meat and potatoes for the after church dinner. This was never a hardship as they had their own beef and pork supply stored away in the locker in town.

This was before home freezers. Actually, they had enjoyed the luxury of electricity only a few months as Rural Electrification had just turned on the "juice." Most of the farmers, including the Evans, had their homes wired for nearly a year waiting for the wonderful event. It was even more difficult for the Evans to wait as they had been used to it and there sat the new refrigerator but no ice box. They did not have an ample supply of kerosene lamps either as they did not want to invest in them since the electricity could come at anytime. It served as a good excuse to not get homework done, which Owen used more than Sarah.

The butchering and locker industry flourished at this time, and while it was a chore to have to go to town to get meat, it was still an adventure for the kids to go into the cold hallways to the family-rented drawer and see all their meat. It was a test of stamina to withstand the cold.

After dinner, the parents visited and the kids were left to find their own entertainment. There were eight of them. It just happened that these families each had a boy and a girl and they were all in their early teens. Owen was the oldest and had a driver's license. Usually these afternoons were spent in outside games, shooting baskets in the hay mow, or just chasing one another around. This day was different.

"If you guys would all decide you wanted to go to the show in Wayne, I bet I could get the car." Owen knew how to bait his peers into action, although Sarah and Owen had long known that they were not to beg for special privileges in front of company.

"We could just be nuisances and they'd let us go."

"Yeh, it's too cold to play outside."

"We could be too noisy playing cards."

"We could just suggest that we would like to go," was Sarah's usual straight-forward way to achieve a goal.

Owen was right about his hunch to get to drive. All parents consented, each kid had his or her own spending money and Griff gladly furnished the car. There was no checking out to see if he had ample liability insurance because if the worst thing happened, they would not go through the courts to solve the problem. They did caution Owen to drive safely. All eight could ride in the roomy family car.

It was the latest Mickey Rooney movie so the Sunday Matinee consumed their interest and time. They were driving home at dusk, ready to join their parents for the supper that would be set out, which would be the leftovers from dinner. Instead of music on the car radio, there were excitable voices giving the news. "Pearl Harbor in Hawaii has been attacked by the Japanese Air Force. The naval warship, *The Arizona*, has been sunk in the harbor and many American sailors went down with the ship. We are awaiting a declaration of war from President Roosevelt."

There was silence and then several spoke at once.

"We'll show those Japanese they can't do that to us."

"What will war be like?"

"It won't bother us, that's a long ways away."

"Boy, I'd go to fight in a war if I was old enough."

"Did your dad fight in the last war?"

"Maybe The League of Nations will stop it like we learned in history."

"America can fight her own battles."

"Japan sure has her nerve to attack us."

"Wonder if our folks have heard the news. They probably haven't even turned on the radio because they were so busy talking."

They rushed into the house, breaking the news as they had guessed right about the radio not being on. Hurriedly, they turned it on, thinking the children could not have heard correctly. Maturity and responsibility made them more awe-struck than the young people, however, they believed that America could solve the problem in record time. They recalled that

World War I had lasted less than a year and a half. Probably each mother thought about not wanting her boy to have to go to war, but was too wise or sensitive to voice concern — sensitive to her son knowing he wouldn't want protection from his mother in a heroic pursuit — wise in not revealing that the first reaction to war was a selfish concern. The fathers, of course, if they thought about the possibility of their young sons going, would have to show pride in their sons fighting for their country. These parents were just kids during the last war, but they were steeped with maternal, paternal, and nationalistic responses. How could twenty-three years of peace impact in this way? It suggests that the maternal and paternal are instinctive, and the nationalistic tendencies come out of the love of the good life as they knew it. The power of socialization was amazing. All four of those young men served in active duty during the four long years of war that followed. And they chose to, even though they could have been exempt for farm work.

No man, woman, or child could have anticipated the changes that took place in their lives over the next four years. The young men went to war, the young girls wrote letters, and the adults led the way in adjusting to shortages. Even mail was different. The girls wrote and received compact messages called "V" mail (for victory) and deeply respected any censored messages in the letters as no one wanted to defy the need for secrecy. A New York address usually meant that the service man was in the European Theater of War and a San Francisco address meant the South Pacific. People back home did not expect to know much more than that. Paper stars pasted on the most visible window of a home denoted how many from that household were serving their country.

Gas rationing was difficult, but people did not complain. An "A" card allowed four gallons of gasoline a week. That was the standard. Special consideration of employment allowed "B" and "C" cards. Doctors, because they made house calls could get the maximum. Factory workers in war plants could also get "C" cards. Because of this, the high school basketball fans and even the team went to out-of-town games to play in a stock truck. It would be clean and a tarp over the top, but the kids brought their own blankets and pillows. Sarah remembered several uncomfortable rides, but would never turn down the chance to go. Of course, Paul's playing on the team had something to do with that. Owen was on that team, too. That was the class of '43. It was the largest class to ever graduate from that small school and it was dominated by males. Most of them went directly into the service. It made one wonder about war coming along when the male population was so high.

Paul's family moved about a hundred miles away after graduation, and he and Sarah had to depend on love letters to keep their romance going. He was going through the process of enlisting, when his family received the sad news of the death of his older brother. He, along with others who had served many missions were killed in a jeep accident en route to the plane flying them home. A war decree stated that if one member of a family gave his life in the service, the others need not serve. Paul wanted to, but was sensitive to his parents' sadness and did not enlist. Being exempt on that basis also prevented his ambitions for officer training or going to college. Only a few "4F" rated men went to college. This meant they were physically unfit, so most of them found some comfort in working in some kind of production work for the good of the war.

Owen enlisted in the Navy, took his "boot training" received an extended length furlough to help with the harvest, reported back to base and was soon assigned to a minesweeper which was his duty for "the duration." Sarah matured. She watched the boys celebrate their leaving by getting drunk. Then when they came home on leave, they would get drunk again. She wanted to understand but was disappointed. She did not join them in the drinking and instead, took on a sort of watchful role. She did tell Owen, without trying to be preachy, "Just try to sober up a little before you get home and stumble through the house. It hurts the folks when they know."

He would retaliate with, "Well, I don't try to hide everything I do. I don't want to be sneaky, even if I'm not proud of what I do."

So that was a losing argument. It was one of those eternally perplexing problems of life. Sarah began as a young person pondering over this type of question wanting to be fair and objective, coming to the realization that there is a very fine line between objectivity and indecisiveness.

She continued to dance with the boys and compliment them on their uniforms. This was not difficult to do as she did like those uniforms. Owen's navy outfit was particularly to her liking as it was to many girls, with the big collar, the jaunty hat and the "P" coat — whatever that stood for. Her favorite was the Air Corps Officer uniform like she saw in the movies. She did not know any officers because her crowd was too young to have had college education before the war started. Besides most of the farm boys were not going to college anyway. Sarah did convince Mary to buy a sailor suit for David before Owen came home on leave. He was so proud to be dressed like big brother, and that made one of the most precious snapshots that was ever placed in the family album.

Sarah was elected to be a cheerleader which suited her personality and physical deftness. She believed in using her energies to support the team, but did not like the rote memorization of yells. The cheerleaders and the Pep Club turned in their orders for kelly green (school color) sweaters early in the fall and waited and waited for them to arrive. Finally the day arrived and as the first sweater was unwrapped and unfolded, an insipid, pale green product was revealed. The sponsor read the enclosed explanation to the disheartened girls, "Your requested color could not be acquired because of the demand for the green dye which is consumed in government issue clothing by our armed forces." The girls were learning not to question the compromises of war, but they never developed any liking for those sweaters. Later, they felt they were not alone, when it was advertised on radio that Lucky Strike green had gone to war. The cigarette packages were plain white where they had been a vivid green. Evidently, the world that seemed to be painted khaki needed green as a base. The girls were somewhat comforted.

In the meantime, the girls held slumber parties in lieu of roller skating and school dances that were so much fun before the older boys had gone away. They took turns driving to the Saturday night double feature at the movies, depending upon what the family needs had been on their gasoline supply. One of the movies would surely be a war story in which airplanes marked with the Japanese rising sun were shot down to go crashing into the sea. The audience in general would cheer its approval and little children learned to "boo" the rising sun emblem. The "Pathe News" was an important feature before the movie began. The viewers then never dreamed that someday they would sit in their own homes and have access to the news and movies on privately owned television.

Another shortage that the farm wives learned to deal with was sugar. This, too, was rationed and the ladies carried their ration books in their purses on shopping trips. Because farmers did physical work, it seemed as though they needed sweets for energy so a deluge of sugarless cake and cookie recipes developed and were exchanged with much discussion. There were some strange textures and flavors, but they were eaten.

The town and city homemakers had meat ration books as well. This was reported to be a hardship that the farm women knew nothing about. All knew of the need to take care of shoes as they, too, were in short supply. There were no new cars produced and people were seen everywhere changing tires using a spare that was better only in that it was holding air for the moment.

There was no shortage on sad, sentimental songs. A new favorite would be at the top of the "Hit Parade" each week. They might move about in the top ten for some time. "Missed the Saturday Dance" told of a lonely girl waiting for her love to come home. "I'll Walk Alone" repeated that sentiment. From the male point of view, it was "I'll Be Home for Christmas" even when they knew they would not be. Claiming loyalty in a humorous tune was "They're Either Too Young or Too Old." And everyone learned the words to "God Bless America" which Kate Smith made as popular as the national anthem. There was unity in America fighting for their common cause, to rid the world of the dictators, Hitler, Mussolini, and Hirohito.

Chapter 28
❧

The graduates of 1944 everywhere knew the effects of war. The young men still wanted to serve their country, but some of the patriotic fervor had changed to fear and obligation. The war had become tedious. Girls floundered, feeling a little guilty in planning college when the fellows could not. They were not yet career oriented. Women had not yet arrived at that point in time. However, the women of the West Coast were working in war plants. That song "Rosie, the Riviter" nudged at Sarah's feelings. She envied them doing something so specifically to help win the war. But she did not know of any place she could go to do that sort of thing. She did not want to get any farther from Paul as she saw him seldom the way it was. He was planning to come for her graduation at which she would be giving the Salutatorian Address. The year before, he had been the Valedictorian and Sarah had been thrilled with his speech. This young love was filled with mutual respect. Although they talked of marriage someday, it was never really imminent. He was farming with his father, but he wanted to go to college after the war.

Owen was off on that minesweeper somewhere and Griff was having a hard time getting hired help, as most of the farmers were. They had thought they would have their sons. Sarah wanted to be of some help with the field work, but after absent-mindedly plowing the potatoes that had just been planted, Griff did not have a lot of faith in her. Another time, the front wheel of the tractor came off while she was watching where the cultivator digs were going. She felt she was not meant to be a farm girl.

Shortly before graduation, the director of the neighboring school, came to talk to Mary and Griff about the possibility of Sarah teaching in their school. They were quick to relay this idea to Sarah.

"You know Sarah, the people from District 55 have their eyes on you for a teacher."

"That wouldn't be doing anything to help the war effort," was Sarah's unenthusiastic response.

"That isn't the way that school boards see it. If they can't get some new young teachers interested some of the schools will have to close."

"Why can't they get some older teachers?"

"Well, they said that if they have any experience, they can teach in town even if they don't have enough college. Just look what happened in high school — Mrs. Becker was recruited when your coach had to go. You can bet any school would be glad to have her. Besides, it was your old history teacher who recommended you, because she is now the County Superintendent."

"She did kind of like me. Wonder what you have to do to teach?"

"The director left this material for you to look at, but all you have to do is pass the teacher exams and go to the Teacher's College this summer."

Sarah had spent enough time stewing over her plans that she welcomed some help and liked the idea of being needed. Her eighth grade teacher, whom she liked, had taken more college hours and moved up to the high school, was just the one to talk to about this. They had become good friends. She encouraged Sarah to take the exams as she remembered how Sarah had worried four years ago and came out fine. Some of the same material would be covered and she would help her review.

Sarah had some misgivings. "How can I teach a country school when I never even went to one. I don't know the first thing about how one teacher can teach eight grades."

"One of the courses at college will show you how to do that and the Blue Book will be your constant companion, that's the curriculum guide."

It did not sound easy and no one told her it would be. Being recognized as capable of handling this job was the key that turned Sarah toward becoming a teacher. The exams were not that difficult and the summer at college was fun. She liked going to classes in those "echoing" buildings and life in the dormitory was much more interesting than life on the farm. There were many of her peers following the same plan and many who were older advancing their education. There were some Air Corps groups on campus, but well separated from civilian teacher classes. Besides, Sarah had eyes only for Paul. He had been able to get to see her a couple of times on campus, and the other girls thought she had the best looking boyfriend around. She did too. In spite of their infatuation with each other, they never compromised their belief that people should be married before being intimate. They had been in the same confirmation class, and it seemed to be a mutual understanding.

Shortly before school was to start, Griff helped her shop for a car. They found a '31 Chevy coupe for $75 that Sarah was quite thrilled with and she applied for and received a B gas ration book. That meant she could get six gallons a week. She was to continue living at home and save most of her money for college next year, or whenever the war was over. She did not have to pay board and room. She was to earn $112 a month. Was she excited! The Board had given the school a general cleaning, but had not checked out the desk. As she was preparing for school to start, she pulled a drawer open and there was a nest of tiny, squirming mice. She slammed the drawer shut, locked the front door and went home. She was sorry for her bargain.

Mary and Griff knew they were going to get pretty involved in their daughter's career. Griff came through on the first challenge. "I'll go over there with you tomorrow and get rid of the mice, and I'll show you how to use sweeping compound on the floor to clean it, and then when it gets cooler I'll show you how to build and keep a fire going in the furnace."

"I didn't know I had to do all those things."

"It's that way with any job. You never know everything that goes with it. We'll have to check the water from the well there and put lime in the outhouses."

Sarah was dismayed. It seemed that all she was getting out of her college education was the privilege to go back in time. If everyone didn't have so much faith in her doing this, it would be easier to back out. There wasn't time to toy with the idea. She pulled the school bell rope on the appointed hour and 17 kids of all sizes bustled into the building. Sarah thought, "Gee, here I am 17 years old and I have that many students and someone in every grade. There won't be a moment in any day that will not be occupied by teaching, except recess and the lunch hour. Of course, I'll be playing softball or "kick the can" then. The first part of the day won't be so difficult, as we'll salute the flag, sing "America," (I'm glad I can play the piano) and I'll read some each day from some good story. Then there is the health check, to see if their hands and fingernails are clean, and a clean handkerchief set out on the desk. I guess it won't be so bad, and the kids were all nice and acted happy to be back in school. I'll especially like to teach arithmetic, spelling, reading and art and history, too. Guess that's about everything except geography, but I can stand that too." This kind of positive thinking, without illusions of grandeur, kept Sarah on track.

As the year progressed, Sarah routinely filled the water can with fresh drinking water, packed her lunch, and drove her little Chevy to school. Mom always saw to it that there was good food to pack for lunch and Dad was always close at hand if the car didn't start or if Sarah needed a little help at the water pump on windy days. The rewards of teaching were soon forthcoming. The two first graders were learning to read and they beamed with their new learning. Sarah felt she did not have a great deal to do with it happening, as every day went by so fast. She taught some procedures the way she had learned, not according to a practiced method, such as sounding out words. Parents and the County Superintendent visited and reported to Sarah that she was doing fine.

That fall, before bad weather settled in, instructions came out telling elementary schools how they could help do something for the war effort. Because Sarah was thrilled with the idea, she could sell it to her students. They hiked around in surrounding areas where milkweed grew, picked and collected the pods. The fine fluffy fiber in the pod was used for insulation in the clothing of the servicemen in the Aleutian Islands. This seemed patriotically fulfilling and it was done with fervor.

The next big project was the annual school program. The students and teacher decided that proceeds would go for wiring the school building for electricity. Most of the farmers had it in their homes by now, so they wanted their school to be up to date. Each child would perform in some way, by speaking a piece, singing, playing the piano, or having a part in a little play. The mothers brought pies to serve after the program. It was great fun even though the proceeds were small. The building of self-esteem and working as a team had immeasurable rewards to those country children in the process of becoming good citizens.

One negative report went far enough to get to Mary and Griff. Someone, while driving by one day, saw one of the students crawling out the window. They decided it best to approach Sarah about this since she had not said anything about discipline problems. When approached, Sarah explained that there was a hornet's nest in the entry way and some of the children were too frightened to go through it. Griff decided that this chore did not come with the job, and it was damaging his daughter's reputation. He went right down to the director of the school board and insisted the nest be removed immediately. It was. It was quite well known in the community, that when good-natured Griff Evans got upset about something, it needed change.

That spring, Sarah's main concern was to be sure her seventh and eighth graders were prepared for the county exams. They were good students, willing to review. It had not been so long since Sarah had worried about those tests and the material had changed very little. They passed with good grades.

That was not the only victory to celebrate in 1945. War ended in Europe. Hitler was defeated and dead. But, the beloved Franklin D. Roosevelt was dead, also. He had been the president for thirteen years. Harry Truman took over the heavy duty of leading our country. A decision about atomic warfare had to be made. The men in the European Theater of War were coming home. Young people were starting to plan their lives again. The bomb was dropped amid much controversy. The only assuagement of national guilt was that it did end the war with Japan, thus saving lives over the long run.

Owen had to continue duty on the minesweeper in the South Pacific. Sarah decided she would go to college. She had been undecided until she and Paul had a misunderstanding. They were supposed to meet in Sioux City for the Fourth of July. She was to ride there with another couple. It rained and the roads were muddy and somehow it seemed there was not a lot of enthusiasm for the trip on the part of the driver. No alternative plan was devised in case things did not work out. He decided not to go. Sarah expected a phone call from Paul, but there was none. Each wrote a letter, which apparently crossed in the mail. Sarah had scolded and suggested Paul might find a girlfriend closer to his home, since she had proven to be too much trouble to treat properly. He complained that he "had looked his eyes out" for them and consequently had ruined a whole day. Those were the first cross words the two had ever had, but the last of their love letters.

"How did she seem after she got the letter?" Griff asked.

"She read it out on the front porch. I knew she wanted to be alone. She did tell me what she had written and what he wrote," Mary answered.

"Now that was a couple of weeks ago. How do you think she is now?"

"She has never said another word about him. She is awfully quiet and her eyes are puffy in the morning."

"I hate to see her looking so sad. Do you think she is excited at all about going to college?"

"She is going through the motions of getting it lined up and planning what clothes she will need. Thank goodness she has that to look forward to and going 175 miles away will help, too. It's easier to have heartaches myself than see my kids go through them."

Her outward appearance revealed that Sarah had learned at age 18, to get on with life and find that ultimately pain eases.

Chapter 29
಄ⵜ಄

Mary and Griff were through corn picking time and still their son was not home. Finally, word came to meet him in Sioux City. Not until they felt his hugs at the train station, did they give their prayers of thanksgiving. Owen could not believe how David had grown. The outgrown sailor suit tallied the length of the war. He was home two weeks and restlessness set in. He came home to farm, but one doesn't start farming at the onset of winter. He wanted to earn money. He had no special skills that were in demand this time of the year. He wondered what the other guys were doing. There were many in the same situation. He wanted to buy a car with his savings, but the few new ones were spoken for and there were very few good used cars as most had been used beyond what they were capable of. He could use the GI Bill to get a college education, but he had no real desire to go. He decided to go to Sioux City and find some kind of work. He and a buddy from high school became bellhops in one of the better hotels. They made good tips without hard labor. They hated to recognize the truth that there was no future in what they were doing. They would decide about farming in the spring. In the meantime, fun was the main pursuit. They had met several girls and found lively nightspots most any night of the week. The city life was charming them away from the farm. The whole world seemed to want to catch up on the fun they missed during the war.

Owen decided to try construction work. There was much new home building and they were paying good wages. That meant working long hours on nice days, and not earning anything in bad weather. Also there were still many shortages on materials as all suppliers had not gotten back to full production yet. It was not the dream job like it sounded in the newspaper ad. Dad's offer to come back to the farm was still good. Griff knew it would take some time for Owen to decide. They worked out a partnership plan, verbally only, to work together. They would share expenses and profit. Owen could buy some calves to raise and get into that operation slowly and surely, the way that Griff had done. Also, Griff purchased the adjoining farm so they could expand.

Owen had a taste for pretty girls. When he met dark-haired, sparkling-eyed Ellen, his marriage partner was chosen. She was young so they waited until she graduated from high school to marry. Owen, his dad, and a carpenter made vital repairs to the newly-acquired farm house. They bought some bright colored furniture, and the house became a pleasant honeymoon cottage.

It seemed ideal, but discord marred the lovely scene. Owen felt his dad was a little too frugal. If they spent more, they could make more. Griff did not see it that way, but he remembered when he did not agree with his dad. The money could not come in fast enough to meet Owen's wants. His young wife could not meet the standards of the experienced farm woman. She tried but was unsuccessful at churning butter, making bread, canning fruits and vegetables. She would get lonesome, staying at home for a few days without going into town. It was a time of transition. The ways of doing many things were changing. Young people wanted life to be easier. Owen heard about the big atomic plant that was hiring in Denver. Getting back to city living had an overpowering pull. They left the farm and moved to that thrilling city on the leeward side of the Rocky Mountains.

Chapter 30
᭠᭠

One of the most unchanged phenomena was the Ladies' Aid, but its participants were not oblivious to what was going on around them. Mary was their president. Conversation went on best while the ladies quilted.

"Mary, have you heard from your kids since they moved?"

Pretending it did not hurt her, she responded, "Oh yes, Owen got the job he wanted. They found an apartment, and they like being in the city."

"That's the way with all the young people since the war. We'll be closing the doors of this church if none of them want to stay around here."

"There's hardly any children in Sunday School now."

"I've seen the time before when we thought that, too. We sound like 'Chicken Little' today, acting like the 'sky is falling down'."

"Well, several of our girls have been to college and they are teaching. Most likely they will marry men in those communities and won't be coming back here."

"What about Sarah, Mary? Will she finish college pretty soon?"

"She will be starting her last year this fall. She wants to teach in high school."

"Does she have a young man that she is getting serious about?"

"From what I hear, it's sort of off and on. I hope she teaches awhile after spending all that money on college."

"I'm changing the subject, but have you heard about how someone with a real bad cold can get a shot of penicillin and feel better right away?"

"That's what they mean by wonder drugs, I guess."

"I can't express how grateful we were when David got an infection from that pin they put in his broken leg."

"My, he did have a time with that leg. Does he still love his pony?"

"Oh yes, we all got such a kick out of the way he trained his pony to put her head down so he could get on and then she would lift her head and he would be in place to ride," Mary explained. "He loves to get us to laugh. Sure is nice to have that imp around with the big kids gone."

"That 'police action' in Korea is making me a little nervous, especially since my boy decided to stay in the army."

"Surely, it can't be as bad as war."

"But it is war by another name."

"We handled Hitler, I guess we can solve that problem in Korea."

"Yes, and we better solve our problems right here. We have to have this quilt finished in two weeks so we can auction it off at our Church Dinner. We have to do our planning for that too." Mary as the task master led her group back to matters at hand.

"What is Griff's idea of making this money for the cemetery anyway?"

"It's called perpetual care. If the Cemetery Association can get enough money saved, then the interest from that money will pay for the care of the cemetery."

"It's a good idea, but how are we ever going to make that much money? I heard he is talking about $10,000."

"Well, we have to start somewhere, and we might as well plan on succeeding."

It was this philosophy that brought dreams to fruition.

Chapter 31
∂∞৶

Sarah was home from college for spring break before graduation in May.

"So you are making applications for teaching jobs?" Griff asked with a pleased look on his face.

"Yes, I would like to get into a class B school. That would be a nice sized town to live in and I would probably have about 100 students in 5 classes in high school."

"It makes us proud that you stayed with teaching. Sometimes, I wondered if we had done the right thing in encouraging you to try that country school," was Mary's concerned response.

"Whatever happened to that boyfriend we heard so much about for a while?" Griff could inquire about this sort of information easier than Mary could.

"Well, he is a good dancer, has a good sense of humor, is one of the best athletes at school, but he is moody. That's when we have our troubles. Besides he has another year of college. Ann and I want to work at Estes Park this summer. Her cousin thinks he can get us jobs. College kids just flock out there for the summer. We both just want to have fun." Ann was her roommate in college. They met as a strangers and became stalwart friends.

"Seems you have a lot of complicated plans, but if you can work them out, that will be fine. Do you have any good chances of getting a teaching job in Nebraska?" Mother was hoping her daughter would not go too far away.

"My best opportunity right now is in Wahoo. Our Placement Center thinks I have a good chance there. That would be close to Lincoln and I could go to my Alma Mater for games and dances. Wouldn't be so far from home either. The bus connections would be pretty good."

"Is your salary going to be much better now that you have a college degree?" Griff felt like his dad, always bringing up the money situation.

"You bet! I was thinking about that, too. I made about $996 that year in the country school and the going rate for a beginning teacher in high school is about $2300 to $2500. So that pays off for me. Guess you don't make any money on your investment, but I sure appreciate getting a college education."

"You know you are the first on either side of the family to graduate from college. We are pretty proud of that and glad we could do it. Farming has been good to us. We'll do something equal for David when he is old enough. We already gave Owen his start." Being fair parents was always a top priority with Mary and Griff.

Graduation was a whirl of excitement for Sarah, including the honor of being in Who's Who. She was so warmed by the nice things that were happening, but she very much wanted to remain humble. She hated bragging and conceit.

The money Sarah had saved had run out at the beginning of her last year. She had bought her clothes and had spending money until then. The folks had supplied her since. Often times Mary would send a formal that she had sewed and Sarah would hem it. That helped, but that year hem lengths dropped about 8 inches. All wardrobes were hurting from that. One favorite outfit Sarah purchased for graduation activities was a black floral print. She complimented it with a black big brim straw hat with a pink ribbon on the crown. She felt sophisticated. Her naturally curly hair helped her maintain a flowing flip and all the girls were concerned about shiny, clean locks. After a shampoo with bar soap, a lemon juice or vinegar rinse gave that desired luster.

During the years at college, the evening meal in the dining room was served by waiters and the students were required to dress appropriately. Sarah enjoyed this; however, it was popular to complain about it. They also had to take turns serving as hosts and hostesses. Sarah was glad that table manners had always been stressed by her mother. They also practiced polite conversation. A vulgar word was probably never expressed at the dinner table. Most of the male students were veterans of the war and had served all over the world. They, too, respected this refinement.

Graduation time was a natural for remembering the strict rules by which most of the students did abide. Freshman girls had to be in the dormitory by 8:00 each week day evening. After the first year, the hour to be in was 10:00. Weekends gave the freedom of midnight curfews and a special permit of 1:00

a.m. was given for certain occasions and had to be cleared through the Dean of Women who also lived in an apartment in the dorm. She stood at the front entrance many nights to check that no one had been indulging in alcohol. There was no drinking allowed on campus. This was difficult to enforce particularly with the veterans. The college men had far more privileges than the women. Very few students had cars on campus. Walking on campus and downtown was the expected way of transportation. The campus included a lake and many romantic paths. Many couples had a romantic start to long and happy marriages. Most of the students took an active part in school activities and acquaintances became long-standing friends. Sarah and most of her fellow graduates felt they had just experienced the best part of their lives.

Ann and Sarah did get their waitress jobs in Estes Park. The school superintendent of Wahoo spent his summers in the Colorado mountains and by arrangement held his last interview with Sarah and had her sign the contract right there in the city park. Certainly, she would have a good year with such an illustrious hiring. The girls found out waitress work could be grueling and appreciated their education even more.

"Ann, let's do something really exciting and fly home in August. We would have to go down to Denver on the bus and then get an airplane to Lincoln," Sarah said enthusiastically since she had a job for the year and savings from the summer job.

Ann was going back to school so was saving in earnest all summer. Sarah had been unusually free with her earnings.

"Well, I would love to do that, but don't know if I should. But, if I want to be an airline stewardess someday, I better find out about flying."

"Now you're talking sense. I know I can never be one because I wear glasses, but you have every chance. Besides, we should reward ourselves for this hard work we've done this summer."

"Have you ever ridden in a plane?"

"Heavens no, when would I have ever done that?"

"That's why we should do it now. A first for both of us!"

"Gee, if I get sick that will be the end of that dream for me."

"Better to find out sooner than later. But I have heard that you can get over it. Just because you get sick once doesn't mean you always will."

"I get dizzy on a merry-go-round. I don't know why I want to do that for a career."

"Probably because it's the most exciting job that has come along for women."

The decision was made. Ann did get sick, and she never became an airline stewardess. However, there were other factors, such as finding her life partner and having three boys to stay home and take care of. Having a family meant not having a career. The daughters of that generation were not so blessed.

Chapter 32
〜∽

Young Miss Evans accepted with enthusiasm some of the sponsorships that the older teachers were weary of, such as the Pep Club. She set up a physical education program for girls, the first that the school had. She introduced girls' basketball rules in which any team member played only one half of the court. They would rather play boys' rules but she insisted on the protection of their health. They learned square dancing and then taught the boys at one of the school dances. She felt good about everything except the mayor's son. He had on two occasions, sworn in the class room. Of course, he was sent to the principal. He in turn reported to Sarah that the boy had a crush on her and just wanted the attention. He suggested that she give him more positive attention. She tried it and it worked. Her one discipline problem finally became a pleasant teacher-student relationship. The other teachers recognized Sarah's serious and conscientious endeavors and accepted her warmly. The superintendent who hired her was supportive and motivated all of his teachers to aspire to their full potential. Sarah respected him immensely.

Sarah arranged for board and room with the widow lady who had the big white house and had other working girls staying there. The charge was sixty dollars a month. She had to borrow the money from her folks as she had spent a little too freely and not saved enough over the summer. Griff had to gently tease her that he thought he was through with dishing out money to her now that she was on the job. All Sarah had to bring were her clothes and her own radio if she wanted one. She spent evenings on school work and visiting with the other girls. There were football games to go to and life was good, but it was an adjustment to be away from the college campus so she investigated the bus schedule and found that she could visit the old school quite readily. Her friends had told her she was welcome to stay in the dorm with them any time. It was like going home.

On her first return visit, while talking with a group of friends at the Student Union who were interested in what it was like to be teaching and earning money, she sensed that Preston was in the room. Theirs was the stormy relationship that she felt she had succeeded in putting in the past. He was walking toward her with that irresistible grin. She forgot what she was telling her audience. Most of them knew that they had had problems, but seemed to recognize they were being drawn together. "Pres," as she had come to call him, asked her to dance. The juke box was playing "Somewhere Over the Rainbow." Evidently, he had arranged that as it had been a special song for them. Whenever they had wished they could run away from finishing college and be married, they had settled for the sentiment that maybe someday dreams would come true. They were alike in that once they started to college, they had great determination to finish. Pres was working his way through and had an athletic scholarship. He was the age of the returning vets, but did not have the advantage of the GI Bill which was a payday every month. He had not been in the service which he told Sarah once and never spoke of again.

"You haven't forgotten how I dance. Gee, it seems good to touch you again. It was about a year ago we broke up. What did you do this past summer? How do you like teaching? Your friends told me you were coming down this weekend. I think some of them want us to get back together."

"I didn't remember you being so talkative."

"But you do remember me and, I hope, how much we wanted to be together in the future."

"It was always so far away, it didn't seem real."

"But look, you're finished and I just have this year left."

"You are different! You were always so gloomy about the time we had to wait. Now you are so optimistic. I could get to like this new you."

"I can see ahead better now, and the future looks bright. I haven't had an asthma attack for a long time. Probably because of being away from the farm. I made good money this summer in Casper. And I never met another girl that could make me forget you."

Other songs were playing now that they took no notice of. Pres pouring out his heart like this triggered a release of Sarah's feelings too.

"You mean we were only about a hundred miles apart this summer. I would often wish that I would look up one day and see you sitting in one of my tables at the restaurant. Ann and I dated lots of fellows this summer, but I never felt a tingle of excitement with any of them."

"That's music to my ears. I'll do everything I can think of to show you I have a bright outlook on life now and maybe you'll love me again."

Back at the dorm that night, the girls wanted to know all about the grand reunion and being hopeless romantics, they were almost as thrilled as Sarah was.

It was agreed that Sarah would return for Homecoming a month away, and that they would write in the meantime. She was still so new to her career that she did not need revitalization for that, but the reborn belief that love lasts through separation was a boon to this young heart that had been so dismayed only four years ago.

The month was too long. After two weeks, Pres borrowed a buddy's car and drove to Wahoo. He drove up beside Sarah as she was walking home from Church. He had inquired at her boarding house as to her whereabouts. He whistled that whistle that proper young girls are not supposed to respond to. But Sarah recognized the voice that said, "How about a ride, Good Lookin'?"

"Oh, how did you know I needed you today?" She did not restrain her feelings.

"I only knew that I needed to see you." He was pleased that his hunches were working right.

Although Sarah was still the unworldly girl she had been at 18, she had a more mature sense of the romantic aspects of life. She thought, "His timing is terrific. I wonder if he'll always have that quality." Maybe she would like to find out.

She would have to go tell them at the house that she would not be there for dinner and she wanted the others there to meet him. They had heard a little of him already.

His suit jacket was a little wrinkled and his shoes were showing wear, but she was proud of his size. Even though Sarah was very slim, she liked the way he made her feel, lithe and feminine. She liked standing on her toes to kiss him.

They were finally alone, riding in the country. "I want to know if you will marry me and if you will, I want to make some plans."

He was being so direct. That was fine, she would be too. "The way you make me feel today, I think we must be right for each other now. If we can put our bad times behind us and just enjoy one another, I really want to become your wife and grow old with you. Feeling this way after being apart for a year is another good sign."

"Yes, yes, yes," and he was kissing her lips, her forehead and her eyelids. "Before we do too much of that growin' old together, I sure want us to do some young things together."

She knew what he meant and thought again that she liked his humor.

Pres wanted to coach high school football, basketball, and track teams. The college coaches were encouraging him as well as the Placement Center. They would hope to get jobs in the same school next fall, as they would be married next summer. Sarah enjoyed the practicality of planning. She did not want to just have wishful dreams. She wanted reality and she and Pres seemed to be more attune now than ever before. Maybe, he could even get into the school where she was now, but usually first year coaches could not start in a school of that size.

The day had been such a turning point in their lives, it was difficult to part. In two weeks they would be together again and they cherished the idea of returning to future Homecoming events for many years to come.

Chapter 33

By Homecoming weekend, Sarah was enjoying being a career woman with a paycheck. She had time during Teachers' Convention to shop for new clothes. She bought a fur coat, three quarter length of luxuriously soft squirrel in a rich sable brown color. Skirts were long so the combination was stylish. Sarah felt elegant. Of course she was faced with more monthly payments, but she understood that responsibility. The Homecoming dance was their statement to the world. Their happiness was obvious and their dancing was its embodiment.

New Year's Eve marked the formal engagement. The diamond was small, but Sarah was thrilled even without knowing that Pres had emptied his bank account to buy it. In the spring, it was known that Pres would not get a job where Sarah was. Her superintendent expressed disappointment that Sarah would not be coming back. It was understood that the man's job was the first consideration. Sarah would try to get a job where Pres could be hired as the coach. While Pres was attending to sending applications, he was not getting anything really accomplished. Mary and Griff were getting anxious about their future son-in-law not having a job, so ventured a little interference. They found that he really had no way to get around to the schools and was too proud to mention it even to Sarah. They made arrangements to take them both to schools where both could be hired, and that was soon accomplished. Sarah did not understand why Pres' parents did not come to his aid, but was glad that hers did. She had met his family only once, just after they were engaged. They were a good deal older than her parents and talked about hard times that Sarah knew little about. This bothered her some, but they were so proud of Pres becoming a college graduate without any financial help from them. There was very little communication between Sarah and Pres on matters such as this.

Wedding plans proceeded. It was to be one of the first "fancy" weddings in that little country church which Sarah joined as a teen and where her grandmother, whom she never knew, had formed the Ladies' Aid. Griff who made few requests, stated very firmly that he didn't want any rented suits at his daughter's wedding. This was respected. Mary and Griff also suggested that Sarah and Pres buy a car with the wedding gift money they were giving them. Until that suggestion, it was unknown how they were going to be able to go on a honeymoon trip. A car was purchased and Pres seemed not to resent the guidance that Sarah's parents were giving. The week before the wedding, however, pent up anger from some unknown source caused Pres to explode with a violent show of temper. He recklessly drove the car out of the driveway, spinning wheels, and stirring up dust. Sarah did not know how to deal with this and was embarrassed.

Wiping away tears she said, "If only we didn't have all the plans made and all of those people coming, I would not marry him."

Mary and Griff were quick to assure her, "Those plans can be canceled much easier than a bad marriage."

About that time, Pres drove back in the yard and came stomping into the house. Griff did not wait for him to state his purpose, grabbed his shirt front looked up at him and told him, "What are you, a spoiled baby or a man? I never saw a man behave like that. I can't let my daughter marry someone with a temper like that."

It was almost as if he had never been confronted about a temper tantrum before. He was instantly contrite. He appealed to Sarah's sense of forgiveness and the plans were kept. Sarah still had some unstated fears in her heart.

Chapter 34
❧~❧

"**D**id we get any mail from the kids?" Griff asked coming in from spring field work to the hearty dinner that he knew Mary would have prepared.

"Well, here is the weekly letter from Sarah, but you know the answer before you ask in regard to Owen."

After reading Sarah's letter, Griff was in an evaluative frame of mind. "Well, Mom, I guess we've done OK by our kids, if David stays on the right path. Sarah's college education makes her a more contented mother, she says. Their life as teachers is a good life even though he doesn't make much money. Owen is glad he had his try at farming, even if it didn't work out. It's taking him two jobs, and those two babies came pretty close together. Before too long, we're going to have to go visit our kids and see the grandchildren."

"So far, it seems they'd rather come home to the farm. Of course, there is a little more room here than they have in their apartments, but I think they still like the country."

"Yeh, Mom, they like your cookin' too," speculates realistic David.

"I suppose you'll find something wrong with staying on the farm too. I wanted to buy another farm, but not much point in that. Got two now. I don't know if I ever want to move to town, but I don't want to work forever. Oh, I could stand to feed some cattle."

"Bet you won't take it easy if you get the chance," David chimed in, showing he knew his parents.

David's high school years went by in a hurry. Mary and Griff attended his basketball games. They had not been able to do that with Owen because of the war. He was also in the school plays and was a "cut up" so fun usually surrounded him. Mary and Griff could keep up with the other parents even though they were older. They never regretted that late offspring.

Even the announcement that he wanted to get married right after graduation was taken in stride. Mary and Griff liked his chosen girl and his idea of living on the other place and getting set up in the Grade A milking plan. They were thrilled that one of the kids wanted to stay on the farm. They were anxious that it be a successful experience before they went off and had a taste of city life. They had to fix a barn to certain specifications, pipe in water and heater, set up the milking machines and buy a herd of good milk cows. A refrigerated truck would regularly pick up the milk and David would get paid on a regular basis. Griff was excited, thinking if a young farmer could know reward for his work in shorter periods of time, maybe more young men would stay on the farm. His own family was indicative of the way things were going.

David's set up was a point of interest to other farmers. He was glad to show his operation. Money was coming in and he pursued a dream; he bought a motor boat. There had been a major hydroelectric plant and dam built about sixty miles from the farm so it was reasonable that these earth bound farmers could actually take up a diversion they never knew before.

Griff reminded Mary, "Gee, that's where we went for our honeymoon, and here these kids today go up there and boat for a day then come home and do their chores."

"A few other things are different too, even though I don't feel we've been married for so long. We didn't have running water in the house and a bathroom when I came here. Guess you are pretty glad you don't have to haul wood into the house. That furnace and deep freeze are pretty welcome there in the basement."

Griff was warmed by his wife's appreciation of their better life and his doing what he thought he was meant to do. He was glad that his young son and family were also reaping benefits from farm life.

When the church needed painting, the men of the church gathered with their equipment that served as lifts, bought the paint and went to work scraping and painting, Griff served as a Deacon so was involved in organizing these activities. The endowment fund for his cemetery project was growing. Mary belonged to the American Legion Auxiliary on the basis of Owen's time in the service. The Woman's Club was another of the satisfying organizations she belonged to as the women pursued informational programs. The Ladies' Aid was like breathing. Bridge club rounded out her interests.

Griff bought a new car quite regularly. He remembered the ordeal of the car that got too old during the war. He became accustomed to driving to Owen's house in Denver and Sarah's house in Indianapolis, but he did not like city driving in general, so Mary and Griff found enjoyment in the planned tours. They would study the tour books and choose a new adventure each year. Their trip to Hawaii was the epitome. They wondered if they deserved such rewards.

Chapter 35
➣❧

"**H**urry girls, we have to get across town to the airport to meet grandma," said the citified Sarah.

"Is Grandma going to stay with us while you and Daddy go to Florida?" asked Connie, the younger of Sarah's two girls.

"You know the answer to that question is yes. Why do you ask what you already know?" stated the efficient older sister, Cathy.

"That sure will be better than that lady that stayed with us last time. She was too crabby," complained freedom loving Connie.

"Yes, I know. I'll have a much better time, too, with Grandma here with you. I can count on you to mind Grandma and show her you appreciate her coming all the way just to be with you girls." Sarah rarely missed an opportunity to teach her daughters values that could not be counted in dollars.

"Why can't Daddy go to that convention without you, Mom?" asks Cathy, sensing additional responsibility forthcoming.

"He likes to have me go and I like to. Besides the company expects wives to go along and that is exactly the way it should be." Sarah respected the large insurance company in which Pres was doing so well. He was one of the youngest managers in the country. The company often recruited coaches with rural backgrounds as they found them ambitious and willing to work.

Sarah had become a comfortable city driver, especially to and from the airport as Pres did quite a lot of flying on business trips. They would be flying to Florida the next day. She was thinking that she hoped Pres would not get overly anxious about his social responsibilities. He felt personally responsible for the agents from Indianapolis to have a good time as it was important to business. His charm was an asset, but quite often it was forgotten when Sarah was the only audience. But she understood that he could not be under that stress all of the time, and knew that he needed her.

Grandma knew that she was wanted and needed by the greeting from her two granddaughters. This became a pattern for several years. Sarah knew she had a special mother and was happy that the miles between them had not prevented a good relationship with her children. One time, when the girls were older, and they lived in St. Louis, they took the train to Omaha. Grandma and Grandpa met them there, and they remember it as one of the best times ever. They went to the movie, "Mad, Mad, World." Then after they got to the farm, Grandma had a hayrack ride and slumber party arranged with some of the neighboring children and their younger cousins, David's two girls.

"Seems like they have better times in the country than we do in the city," observed outspoken Connie.

"Yes, and everybody knows everyone else and they are so friendly," recognizes cautious Cathy.

"It's even fun to go to that country church." Sarah remembered the first time she went to it at about the same age as Cathy and felt as though she was claimed. Could it be that her children needed that as much as she did?

"They don't have to make reservations every time they want to go somewhere, either."

Pres' grimaces indicated that his daughters were not happy with the life he was providing. It hurt him and he became defensive about it as he did so readily over unintended remarks. But he had other worries. There was that company physical that showed questionable shadows in his lungs. He had given up smoking, but maybe not soon enough. One doctor said it is not so complicated to remove a portion of the lung. Preston knew he would not survive that so did seek another opinion. This expert had another diagnosis.

"I would bet my professional image of high standing on the premise that you do not have lung cancer. The fear of cancer is doing you more harm than what you have in your lungs. It is simply hystoplasmosis, not too uncommon in the midwest region of this country."

"Well, what about my throat and my shoulder pain. I know I'm just filled with cancer and you are trying to convince me that I am not because you can't operate on it."

"We'll put you in the hospital, take a biopsy of your lungs, remove your tonsils, (they are infected) and convince you that you are in good general health."

"I doubt that, but when do we get started?"

A series of tests and numerous periodic x-rays followed and still Preston was not soothed. Other doctors prescribed tranquilizers and anti-depressants. He worried about making

the quota each week. He cried on Sunday night before the new
week started and on Thursday night knowing the totals on
Friday would be insufficient. And yet the home office had no
complaints. It was the best the St. Louis office had performed
for years.

John F. Kennedy was shot. The country mourned the loss
of its young President. Preston was sure it was a conspiracy
against Kennedy saying "You can't trust anyone. The higher
you go up the ladder, the worse it is. I think someone wants me
out of the company."

"But Pres, Dear, how can you think that when all the
home office people are so supportive and pleased with your
production," Sarah vainly attempted to reason.

"Talk is cheap, and it's easy for you to believe because you
don't have to meet a quota every week."

It was wasted effort for Sarah. She was becoming discouraged. She knew that if any decisions were going to be made
about their future well being, she would have to make them as
Preston was irrational. Still she needed to see his responses to
her suggestions.

"Dear, we need to get you away from the pressure of
business. It's breaking your spirit."

"I have a family to support and what else can I do?"

"You could take up teaching again. You often mention
that good and simple life."

"Ha, we couldn't live on a teacher's pay after we've become accustomed to this lifestyle."

"I could teach too and we could make do. I've been thinking that I need more to life than playing Bridge and planning
dinner parties."

"Why, I can't let you go to work. Think how that would
make me look — like a failure which I am."

"I can look into how we could get recertified, that would
be a start."

"You can try, but it won't do any good. I'm not going to
waste my time."

Even though he was negative about any plan, she felt she
had sensed some plausibility in returning to their original profession. Of course, they would have to go back to Nebraska to
carry out this hope, so Sarah began with state requirements for
recertification. It would take a summer program at their Alma

Mater. That could certainly be done. The big question involved the timing on when to hunt for the jobs, before or after summer college. They were getting so much assurance from the college that plans would work, they decided to send letters of application ahead and follow up with personal interviews while the girls had spring vacation from school. At this point, Preston was functioning rather well and was helpful. It was as if he saw some hope in getting out of the maze in which he was entangled. It was still difficult to him to take any rejection such as the positions have been filled or we need someone who can teach a different combination of subjects.

As they were diving into Sumnerville on the tree-lined main avenue, Cathy said, "This would be a nice town to live in." This was from a girl who was attending a city high school of 2400 students.

"Look at that park over there with all the pretty flowers and the swimming pool. That looks neat. Oh, Dad, look at the golf course. Drive around that lake to see it better."

Preston made a quick turn at the mention of a golf course and mused, "Doesn't look too bad."

Sarah was so pleased with the pleasant responses. Cathy had been reluctant to think about moving as she had a circle of friends and a boyfriend. Adults tend to dismiss the importance of that first love, but Sarah remembered how important hers was. The girls waited in the car while Sarah and Pres kept their previously arranged interview. The Superintendent turned them over to the Principal to show them the facility. School was in session so kids and other teachers were watching and surmising what was going on. In small towns most happenings are of public interest. The interview would be continued after lunch as the officials were to have lunch at their Rotary Meeting.

Reverting to his paranoia, Pres fretted, "They are not interested. They're just trying to put us off before they tell us the bad news. Gee, I think I could have gotten to like this place."

"I didn't get that feeling at all. I think they just expect us to believe them. Anyway, we are going to be there to complete the interview. The most difficult thing for them to believe is why you are wanting to leave the fine job you have. Better be ready to give convincing reasons for wanting to leave the city. Don't emphasize pressure of the job, because no doubt they feel their jobs have it, too," Sarah preached as she regained her intensity about solving this problem.

"OK, OK, I'm not going to blow it, have a little confidence in me."

"How many kids go to this school, Dad? It doesn't look very big. Probably doesn't have a Home Ec department or an Art teacher," worried Cathy.

"They said there were about 100 students in each of the four classes and they do have both Art and Home Ec. I asked because I know you both are interested," Pres responded showing more caring than the girls sometimes realized.

The beautiful April day and the budding trees made the waiting somewhat easier for the girls, but so much was at stake. They knew when they saw their Dad's smile that all had gone well. A gentleman's agreement was made that both would be hired in positions in which they would be qualified and certified. The written contracts would soon follow. Anxieties had given way to satisfying planning.

Before leaving town that day, they found that there was a subdivision with available building lots in a desirable part of town close to school and the Country Club. Their combined salaries would equal about half of Pres' salary, but Sarah was sure they could work out finances with very little sacrifice and relieve much of the stress in their present situation. There were many things to do when they got back to St. Louis, but first they would finish out the vacation time by driving the 75 miles to the farm to tell "the folks" (Mary and Griff) the exciting news. They were coming home to Nebraska!

Mary and Griff were more emotional than Sarah expected. She had spent herself on the problems that they had been having and not noticed the loneliness expressed in her mother's letters since David and his family had moved away from the farm.

Chapter 36

Sarah felt guilty for having been oblivious to the problems of others. She thought that David had been lured to the city just as Owen had been, but there had been heartache, too.

The milking operation of which he had been so proud was the basis of it. The milk supply from the cows continued to wane. David thought he was taking good care of his equipment and his herd, but there was a flaw in the milking machine. It did not adequately drain the cows' udders which in turn caused them to give less milk. He was faced with buying a new milking herd and new equipment. He had learned a new trade in the process of trying to make a go of it on the farm. He could move to Denver where his older brother was and get paid a good hourly wage with his new skills in a print shop. He was tired of trying to outwit cows and machines. He would not sell his boat as that part of his life was too dear to his whole family to give up. David's wife who had been proud to be a farmer's wife was by now as anxious as he was to make the change to city life. Their children, three girls and one boy, had become very close to Mary and Griff and they missed them.

"Well, Mary our kids sure are restless. Must be the times. They sure don't take after us, but on second thought we had our moves too," conjectured Griff out loud.

"We can't say too much, but it sure does seem like a lot of dissatisfaction. It seems like our reasons for moving were more real, like having an income to put clothes on our backs. These young people today talk about pressure and fulfillment. That never entered our minds."

"Well they don't run away from debt and they aren't lazy because it takes energy to make those changes. What do you think about Sarah going back to teaching?"

"She seems excited about it. Maybe that college education makes her feel she has to do something beyond the home. I guess I never felt that way. I just felt tired after the rush years. She has been living a pretty soft life the last years. It won't hurt her."

"It will be nice to drive to see them without going to a big city. We can enjoy our granddaughters more."

"Actually, we just traded cities to drive to because now David's will be in the city. Just so we can keep some of them close by."

Sarah's girls seemed to adjust quickly to small town life. Cathy got a part in the Senior play which recognized a speaking ability which she did not know she had. It gave her a new confidence that she would probably never have achieved in that large high school. Although Connie's singing voice had been recognized before, it had not been so important as winning ribbons at music contests and being a part of a team. Pres and Sarah found their new duties challenging and rewarding. Pres particularly liked driving four blocks to school instead of the long morning and evening trips on the freeways to and from his office in downtown St. Louis. They joined the country club that had a sporty golf course and felt accepted on their own worth, rather than their fiscal worth. Their new home was spacious and comfortable. Pres and Sarah found investing much of their own work in it did add to owner satisfaction. They joined the other teachers, most were younger, in after game coffees. Pres told the story so many times as to why he left the city, he had come to believe it. It was based on getting away from the smog and the rush way of life and getting back to basics. Sarah wearied of the story because she knew the deeper truth. However, it did seem as though a solution to their problems had been found, if they just did not get into those arguments about some debatable theory or contextual meaning of words.

David's work in the print shop was paying well, but he had a chance to buy into a business that he could work in the evenings. He could add a good deal to his income. They soon purchased a home and the business grew. The business required more equipment than he could park on his driveway, so a shop for repair and parking purposes was added. Soon the hourly pay job was given up. As repairs were a constant in maintaining the trucks, David and his "buddies" started to build a race car in their spare time at the shop. David put up the money for the parts and drove the car in the races. This became a way of life that he loved. The cars became higher powered and higher priced. The country boy was racing the tracks of Denver in a car that he built with the money from a business that he built. His wife, Joan, was his greatest fan, and would pack up the four children and take them to the races on Saturday night. The car and the sport did not seem to spawn jealousy but unsolicited attention from women who idolized race drivers was not welcomed by Joan as would be the response from most wives.

When Mary and Griff visited Denver, of course they divided their time equally between the two families of their sons. The children coaxed them to go to the races and see Daddy drive. Griff kind of enjoyed it, but Mary said, "I can't call that much fun, sitting there afraid of a crash at any moment. David, it seems to me you could find a safer hobby than that."

"But mom, these cars are safer than regular factory built cars. They have roll bars and a stronger frame. Besides, I wear a helmet and a fire suit."

She was not convinced, but for years asked him how he did in the races. On one occasion, he reported that he had lost his engine.

Mary, in a quick literal interpretation said, "Well you could surely find it on that big open track." This became their private joke and a source of understanding for both of them.

The relationship with David and Joan's children was still close, since they had that good start when living on the adjoining farm. Their only boy was spunky, and reminded Mary of David when he was little. He was always well behaved when Mary kept him for some reason. Mary and Griff treasured that precious time with those grandchildren. They were the only ones that they had the joy of living close to in those early bonding years.

Big brother Owen lived across town and was so busy with his own business, as it too was flourishing, that he rarely got to the races. His wife, Ellen, was chief bookkeeper, and a busy mother of five. Billing and collecting were rarely finished from one month to another. When Mary and Griff visited, Mary would help out by preparing the meals. Besides Owen would remind his mother how much he missed homemade bread. That was all he needed to say to motivate Mary. As a boy at home, he contended he could smell home baked bread the minute he came over the last hill.

Owen's family was fun loving and jolly. They enjoyed their grandparent's visits as they knew they were special to them.

The youngest one seemed to have the knack of getting to his grandma. He would dig in the kitchen cupboards and come to her with, "Here Grandma, here's the blue 'namel pan to make some good meat and gravy."

Mary's whole family knew the value of a blue enamel roaster for the best tasting, tender roast with juice enough for gravy that could not be matched. She had given most of them one at a wedding shower or house visit.

Owen and Ellen were the kind of parents that allowed growth of the individual. Griff recognized this quickly, when upon one of their visits, they were graciously given one of the girl's bedrooms complete with a round bed. He artificially grumbled, "I don't know how you can wake up in the morning without being dizzy, sleeping in that bed."

All children seem to need that unconditional acceptance which Mary and Griff were able to give to all their grandchildren.

The laundry and office work were forever needing attention. Mary applied her natural organizational skills to the housework. This made her feel needed and helped Ellen catch up. Mary surmised from all the checks she carried to the bank, that their business was doing fine. She knew too, from some conversation with Owen, that there were many expenses to running a business. Income taxes were a constant concern, besides insurance for their employees, and the employer share of Social Security. Mary and Griff did not see how Ellen could do it all. Owen comforted them with the assurance that he had an accountant to consult regularly.

Chapter 37
∂∼∽

The long, tedious, Vietnam War was brought to a close. Our country's attitudes had been devastated. Almost any comment was an understatement. The salt had lost its savor. Repercussions were many and diverse. For some, it was deep and painful reasoning. Long-held values were changed. Plaguing questions were being asked. "Why did the war last so long? Why is it over and we have no victory to celebrate? When do we let the draft dodgers come back from Canada? What can we do about the drug problem? Why shouldn't abortion be legal? Why can't anyone get a divorce if he or she wants one? What's wrong with sex between two consenting adults? Who says men can't wear their hair long? Why go to church? Who cares how rough our language is? Why get married? Why be monogamous? What makes the last generations think they know how it should be? They brought on this mess."

These were the conditions under which most of Mary and Griff's grandchildren were raised. Would the parenting skills their children knew be adequate? Those skills were, for the most part, the ones that Mary and Griff used in vastly different times.

Pres and Sarah were glad of their earlier decision to move out of the city. Pres was stern and Sarah gentle, but the combination worked quite well. Sarah would sometimes want to protect the girls from Pres' irritation and other times she depended on it for support. After a happy graduation and a summer job, Cathy eagerly went off to college planning to major in Art or Home Ec. Enrollment was at an all time high since attending college excused military service. Cathy soon met and married a young man, Todd, who just missed the "hippie" influences and planned to get into education. Pres could see him going into a job with bigger money. He was a "go-getter." Their wedding was lovely; Cathy sewed a fashionable bride's dress and Sarah and Mary made the food for the reception held at their home, inside and out. The patio was Pres' pride as he hauled the bricks and fitted each one into his desired pattern. He poured champagne and accepted compliments. He was the gracious father of the bride. This traditional affair indicated that they had escaped the societal pulls so far.

Owen's oldest boy came home from the "police action" with the scars that many did, drug experimentation and disillusionment with the future. He was vulnerable and met and married the wrong woman. Owen and Ellen were patient and supportive of him as they knew they had a kind and sensitive son. His younger brothers and sisters were in a way, victims of the crowded Denver schools. These circumstances do not motivate children. This same thing was happening to David's children.

Sarah's Connie kept her straightforward personality plus a tendency to be idealistic. She joined the masses of students who trailed their respective college campuses with frayed hems on their jeans, but was disappointed with her peers when they scoffed at old values. Expressing herself in art was a saving force. She could paint, sculpt, and shape clay on the wheel turning out creations that were colorful, unique, and free spirited. The two girls' wedding spanned that decade of the Seventies. Changes had taken place. Because there was no longer a family home and patio, Connie planned a wedding that softened that grim reality, and spared her parents from guilt. Amidst an artful setting, under a latticed arch, Connie and her good-looking groom, stated the traditional vows. They emerged from unsettling times, dedicated to those vows and traditions in choice of profession and raising of their family. The groom, Richard, chose order in his life to the point of becoming a successful lawyer.

Chapter 38
ɔↄ⌢

*T*he times had very little to do with Pres and Sarah's divorce. It is true that it was made easier by the new "No Fault" law. They had no difficulty claiming irreconcilable differences. They tried counseling; it delayed matters for a year but solved no problems. Sarah felt that she had spent her wisdom, heart and soul to avoid this catastrophe in their lives. The moving from the high pressure job in the city was supposed to put Pres at ease. Nothing could seem to give him that peace. The quarrels that erupted between them seemed to be founded on competition. It had been a terrifying view of himself for Pres to allow Sarah to share the responsibility of their livelihood. He needed her to be strong and successful, but wanted her to be dependent and less successful than he was. He seemed to resent the interest and cooperation she received from the students. He could not discuss the day's happenings without feeling that Sarah was hunting for something for which she could criticize. Any show of interest in his subject matter, history or economics, in which Sarah had always held interest, was regarded as nosiness as to what he was teaching. If Sarah and the girls stayed up after he had gone to bed, he thought they were discussing him. Paranoia was ruining their search for happiness. The idealistic Sarah could no longer endure violent words and hurting attitudes. She filed for divorce. A difficult year ensued. Each sought separate housing and the home in which they planned to grow old together, was sold.

Their colleagues, neighbors, and parents were shocked. At least, they had not made their problems open information. After filing, Sarah emptied her heart to Mary and Griff.

"I always thought divorce was a disgrace, but now I have to see it as a blessing," was Mary's response.

Sarah felt understood by her family, but could not presume that Pres' family would understand. They had always viewed Sarah as a supportive wife, and knew Pres went through difficult emotional times. Sarah had not expressed her hopelessness to them, so they could not know the magnitude of their problems. She did not want to think what it would be like to no longer be a part of that family of which she had become so fond.

Cathy and Connie were aware of the strife between their parents. Cathy lived five hundred miles away, had one child and another due in a few months. She despaired at the idea of not having a home to go to for holidays with a happy Grandma and Grandpa. She wanted for her children what she had known as a child. Sarah wanted that too, but could not seem to make it happen. Connie had heard too many of the quarrels. She did not hold sentimental ideas at that time about the happy household.

On the occasion of the first time that Sarah and her daughters were together after the filing, Sarah was intent on one message they must receive.

"You must accept and know in your hearts, that your father and I loved each other and wanted each of you from the moment you were conceived. The sad outcome of this marriage is not your fault or from the lack of love in the beginning."

"I accept that, Mom, but what happens to love?" Cathy was no doubt fearful of her own marriage.

"I've asked myself that question many times. The best analogy I can think of is the way car tires wear out. It's friction, constant friction. We've had too much friction for love to survive."

"Thanks, Mom, for caring that we knew that. I'll try to remember when my resentments flare up," Connie vowed.

The desolate threesome stood there hugging and weeping.

Pres, too, was hurting and bewildered. He never seemed to realize what he did wrong, and felt he had always tried to please Sarah. He did admit to some unkind remarks in a diary that was left open on the kitchen table and bemoaned harsh words to his dear love. He could not orally repeat these thoughts. At one point, he sent a note to Sarah with his wedding ring enclosed. It was the first time he had removed it in twenty-four years. That nearly broke Sarah's determination to see this thing through. Almost simultaneously, he would be particularly difficult about some of the business matters that had to be settled and that would stay Sarah's resolve.

As the year ensued, Sarah knew that they caused discomfort for the other teachers in the building and at social affairs. She knew one of them must leave that precious little town, and it seemed that she would be the one.

Chapter 39
∂∽↩

Sarah was not exempt from the ambivalence that accompanies divorce. At times, she felt fortunate to be free and other times grieved over not being a married woman. The new title for women, Ms., meant to avoid revealing marital status in those woman-liberating times, spawned a poem from Sarah.

Most of the time Ms. suggests sophistication,
A woman at home in the real world,
An exciting career,
Clothes in vogue,
Satiny trench coats and fashion boots,
Flights on 727's.
On another day Ms. seems nothing more
    than a woman
Who is nobody's Mrs.,
And more amiss than a Miss.

Sarah recognized her own pain in the poem, but also knew her desire to make the transition by enjoying her new freedom. She had been serious long enough and had tried to seek answers to problems that refused to be resolved. She was going to get with the times.

She even decided on a career change if that's what it would take. She would move to Triumph. Surely there would be opportunities there. She did keep her senses enough to go job hunting before moving. Triumph was "Boom Town USA." New malls were being finished. Stores were opening and trade was coming in from a large surrounding area. Business conferences were held at the local motels which were also expanding. Horse racing was a big attraction. Live music and dancing was the action at every night spot in town. Traffic on the "strip" was hectic.

While Sarah was signing up at the employment agency, a call came in for a personnel manager at a retail store. Her credentials seemed to be adequate; she had a job after being in town 24 hours. She had much to learn, but was finding a new confidence and enthusiasm to meet the challenge.

Sarah had never seen a time clock, but now she was keeping track of hourly pay and overtime, since it was now her responsibility to keep the wage budget in accordance with the sales of the store. She also hired, fired, scheduled and supervised. Morale of the employees was important. This was a natural sensitivity to Sarah and her boss, who was younger than she was, seemed to be pleased with what she did.

She found a nice new apartment as that, too, was a result of the building boom, but her nice new car had to sit outside, one of the prices of divorce. They had always had a double garage. Mary and Griff were anxious to see her new home, her office with no window, but her name on the door, and this huge store with all its bargains. Connie was going to a summer session at college, but came with her grandparents. Grandpa had taken care of her dog since the family breakup, but she could stay on the farm over the weekend, unlike living in town. It wasn't much later, that the favorite cocker spaniel died and Griff buried her out by the hay barn. Connie always knew her Grandpa had done right by her beloved pet.

The new job was fun but tiring. The lure of the night spots took up an empty evening, now and then, for Sarah. She found out there were plenty of men wanting to dance, and why shouldn't she accept? She went out more. She made some "party pajamas" that were as gaudy as the times, and danced and enjoyed this irresponsible popularity. She was not looking for a husband; she had broken that promise once. Beneath her gaiety, there was disillusionment. She had some clever lines such as "I don't like to make long commitments, not anything over ten minutes." She soon found out that many other people were experiencing divorce and many more marriages were in trouble. She learned that men thought they were flattering a woman by asking for her phone number. Out of the pride that she was not sitting home waiting for any phone call, she would give her number and say, "It self destructs in a week." While Sarah was learning to cope with the world she was now a part of, she was becoming independent and non-judgmental, but superficial and a trifle haughty. She seemed to attract men and that seemed to be the all important goal. Her defenses were good. They could not hurt her. If they were irritable, serious, or demanding, it was a simple matter of being too busy for a date.

And then, just minutes out of one of those carefree evenings changed Sarah's invulnerability. She met a tall, slim, gray haired man who gently bent toward her as if every word she said was significant. When she was telling him where she worked he interrupted with, "I know where you work. I've seen you come from the back of the store to the courtesy counter, put announcements on the board, and go over the work schedule for the girls who work that counter."

"You are describing my job exactly, but I can't figure out how I didn't see you. I don't usually miss seeing a good looking man."

"You were so busy tending to your duties, you weren't looking around. I sort of admired that."

Sarah had the feeling that this man would never again be in her presence without her awareness. They danced close and then apart to provide that glimpse of whatever the eyes might reveal about the strange intensity existing in their clasped hands. Words were sparse. Sarah restrained the desire in her fingertips to trace his brows and the lines to his thin lips and stable chin.

"I'll see you again next week when I'm in town. I see us having a long relationship."

Sarah thought, "He really takes charge." She had liked that quality in Pres and wondered quickly why he lost it.

"I know how to get in touch with you."

She liked that he did not have to ask for her number, and she knew she would be waiting for his call. There was so much she wanted to know.

He kept his word that following week. "What I have to tell you, I want to tell you face to face, and the sooner the better."

Sarah recognizing his tenseness, immediately agreed and invited him to her home. She sensed disheartening news.

He stepped in the door and proceeded with his mission. "I should have told you right away that night we met. I am married. I feel like a fool talking about a long relationship when you didn't know the situation. All I knew was I wanted to see you again and again."

"Hello Darlin', I'm married would not have been soon enough," Sarah responded with hurting laughter in her voice and tears running down her face.

"I'm sorry. How did it get so complex in such a short time?"

"You married guys shouldn't be out on the town like that." Sarah had to speak in short sentences to keep some control.

"I wasn't out looking for a one night stand. You know that because that didn't happen. That bunch of guys I was with just came in for a drink or two after our all-day seminar."

"Single women are such easy prey."

"I didn't intend to get involved with you. It happened natural and easy."

"Do you feel involved with me?"

"I guess that's why I am here. I didn't pursue you that day I saw you at the store, but when I saw you again it seemed like we were being thrown together."

"Why are you so susceptible if you are married?" Sarah was a hard interrogator. It was natural for her to get to the bottom of issues.

"Tough question. My wife is a good woman, we raised three children. I didn't finish high school because I joined the Navy the last year of the war. We were married as soon as I came home. I have a good job now, but it wasn't always that way and she didn't complain. She worked too when necessary. I don't want to betray her. We've become very distant in the affection department. Guess you could say I'm lonesome in my marriage."

Sarah had heard these tales of woe before, but this time she was deeply touched. Everything he said had the ring of truth. "You say you don't want to betray her and yet your being here now is a step in that direction. I don't want to betray my principles either. Why am I so close to it? Because I met someone who has affected me in a way that I had forgotten about. I guess it is the same way for you. We must not give in to these feelings. We would regret it for the rest of our lives."

"I know you are right. Better to 'nip it in the bud.' It will be awfully hard to forget. I'll leave you now."

Sarah experienced a profound sadness. It was one more time that natural feelings did not lead down the path to happiness. She would quit going places where she would want a dance partner. She would have to pray for strength and direction.

Chapter 40
༺≺✑✑⥾

Exciting plans were being made in the recently remodeled Evans' farm home. It was warmly decorated and comfortably air conditioned. It represented fifty years of love that grew and evolved as life demanded in Mary and Griff's marriage.

"We'll have the reception at the Community Center, the supper at Church, and the program and dance back at the Center. Do you think that is too much running around for our guests?"

"No, I sure don't. Four or five miles don't mean a thing these days. It isn't like it was fifty years ago. But Mary, you can't do all the work getting all the food ready. Get those people that fix dinners at church. And you don't have to worry about saving every penny you can."

"Well, I want things nice. I'm going to wear a new long dress and you need to get a new suit. Then we are going to get that band that is popular around here right now. You have to tend to that."

Griff knew he was in for some hectic days of carrying out Mary's plans. She was a stickler for details.

"I'm glad that Sarah, Owen and David are going to be in charge of the program. They are going to do an imitation of "This Is Your Life," you know that TV show everybody used to watch. Hard tellin' what they'll come up with. And by the way, we aren't serving any form of alcohol at the dance."

"Well now, Mary, you know there will be some there. We can't control that."

"But, we don't have to be a party to it."

All the children and grandchildren were present at the glorious event. Mary happily exclaimed that she danced with her husband, her sons, her grandsons, and her three year old great grandson. Owen and David danced with their spouses. Sarah was conspicuous in being alone. A close friend of David was sensitive to this and came to her rescue for the first dance for the family. David and his wife were less than congenial to each other, and Owen's first grandchild was with his single mother, the father having given his name only in a very brief marriage.

"There were lots of compliments on our celebration, and I do think people had a good time," Mary analyzed.

"How about us, we had a good time, too, dear wife of fifty years. I was kind of surprised that you like that song, "Honeymoon Fever," so well. David did a good job of singing that and he looks like that guy that sings it on TV."

"Yes he did, and I'm so proud of our children, but they all seem to be experiencing too much pain in their lives. Is it the times?"

"But they act happy and seem to be able to take whatever happens to them. I guess maybe we can take a little credit for that. We got through some rough times. The world isn't as hard on people and their mistakes as when we were young. In a way, that's an improvement."

"Sometimes I blame the cities. They don't know their neighbors and that might appear as not being nosy, but it's really just not caring. I think our children would have had better lives if they had stayed right here in our community and married Welsh kids," recognizing the Welsh influence in her life.

"Well, I have wished that, too, and I would like to see my sons be farmers. But there is no use crying over spilled milk." Strangely enough, old adages proclaimed wisdom and people like Mary and Griff had learned to live by them.

David had taken his big sister in his confidence and revealed that divorce was in the near future. He had put off the announcement until after the Golden Anniversary celebration was over.

"I know I can talk to you, Sis, because you have been through it. If Janet and I go anywhere expecting a good time, something happens to make her mad, then we come home and quarrel about it. I know I upset her and do things to make her jealous, and about the time I decide I'm not going to let it happen, then she does some flirting and makes me mad. We don't make love, we make hate. I can't take it."

"I know Janet feels trapped in your home and that the whole family takes her for granted. She doesn't feel appreciated being secretary for your business. I suggested she get a job away from home and let you hire a secretary. That didn't go over very well. You do have some serious problems."

"I need her help. She has always been so smart with math and reading. When I tell her, she thinks I am just 'buttering her up'."

"I would certainly have preferred to stay married, but I couldn't take the consternation. I hope the outcome will make you happy, whichever way you two decide to go. Let me know so that if it is divorce, I can be with the folks when they get the news."

Their decision was "irreconcilable differences," the new phrase of the Seventies that grew out of the "no fault" divorces. Oh, that they were as painless as the law so intended. David notified his parents by phone, and Sarah went to see them for a solemn visit. She knew they would despair over the odds of two out of three children getting divorced.

"What did we do so wrong?" was the ultimate question from both Mary and Griff.

"With all my heart, I believe you did nothing wrong, unless it is wrong to have people believe in love. All three of us kids had the right to expect to fall in love, get married, have a family, and last forever together. Your marriage was our best example and it survived difficulties. David and I just couldn't make it work out that way."

Not being easily soothed, Mary and Griff shook their heads in remorse.

"Another consideration which you had nothing to do with, is the idea that people should not stay in unhappy marriages, and that for children to see their parents quarreling is harder on them than divorce. I'm not sure that it's true, but it is widely accepted modern psychology."

"Modern law has made it too easy to end marriages, but I was glad that you did not have to go through any more than you did. The Judge was cross and you look frightened, sitting there in that courtroom."

"Furthermore, I would have had difficulty getting a divorce, because we had no third or fourth parties involved. The new law does recognize that relationships flounder and fail."

Sarah had become quite verbal in discussions of this type. This was her style — talk things out, deal with the worst case scenario and the actuality may be not as severe.

Chapter 41
❧❧

The country telephone system was improved over the one Griff hesitated to use fifty years ago, but it still was not private enough for the conversation taking place.

"Dad, this is Owen. I have been hinting that I was having some financial problems. Well, my trucks need repair and I can't borrow any more money. I don't know how things got into such a mess — I've had an accountant all along. Anyway, can I borrow some money? It's coming in all the time. I just need to allocate it a little better, and I can start paying it back right away."

"Well, I'll have to talk to Mom about it, but I suppose we can help you out. How about writing a letter after you know how much you need and we can work out a repayment plan." Griff was uncomfortable with this kind of discussion on a party line. Besides, it was hard to talk feeling so sorry for his son.

"I was afraid of something like that happening," mumbled Mary, "but we can't say no."

"I don't know how they can pay back if they are having trouble, but maybe they have learned a good lesson. They just can't let bills pile up. Good thing they don't have to depend on the rains coming the right time in their business."

More phone calls had to be endured and the bargain was made based on regular monthly repayment.

Griff was coming down with one of his terrible winter colds. Mary always blamed his respiratory weakness on his stint of working in the mine. Instead of the usual pattern, the cold seemed to require a doctor's attention. Mary drove to town with Griff as the passenger. The doctor insisted he be hospitalized in Sioux city and that Mary drive him there immediately.

"I can't drive to Sioux City and go over that bridge. It scares me even when Griff is driving."

"You'll do it if you care about your husband."

She guessed she could do it and did. She also made arrangements to stay in the city close to the hospital. Sarah came to visit and was alarmed enough to call her brothers to come see their Dad. Before they arrived, Sarah had the opportunity to tell Griff that he had been a good Dad. She had never talked to her dad in glowing terms and wasn't going to start now. "Good" was actually an understatement. She didn't know how he could have been any better.

"I've always appreciated my college education. Your being a successful farmer provided that for me."

"I should have gotten another farm so I could leave one for each of you kids after Mom is through needing them."

"Oh, Dad, don't be worrying about that. You have done very well and we're not through with you yet."

The boys flew into Sioux City directly from Denver. They were jolly. Their spirits were uplifting. Griff seemed to be warmed by his family's devotion and his condition improved enough to be released, however, his health never returned to normal.

Griff had decided several years before that he would retire from the work of farming, but did not want to move to town as many farmers did. Mary had longed for that one new house to enjoy in a lifetime, but when decision time had come, she was just as satisfied to stay in their old comfortable farm home.

Anyway, she didn't know what Griff would do in town. There was always something to putter with out in the country.

The land was rented out on a crop share basis, so that needed supervision. He kept some cattle that could graze on pasture land, thus avoiding the plague of chores at a regular time each day. Griff had not adopted all the new farming techniques such as contour rows, but kept a close watch to avoid erosion. Alfalfa, which was a regular harvesting project, was now handled by a company that just came to pick it up and take it to a dehydration plant. Farming had never been easier.

But the payments from Owen were not arriving regularly as planned. Griff offered an extension.

"Dad, I really appreciate the offer, but I can't make it even with that help. I'm in so deep that I have to declare bankruptcy. Never thought I'd do that to the Evans name. I'm sorry." His voice broke and silence ensued.

Griff's aged but optimistic spirit came through at this disconsolate moment, "Son, you're young, you can climb back up there again. You can still have a good life."

"Thanks Dad, I never want to operate at that size again, but I'll provide for my family some way. I won't let you be completely ashamed of me."

Griff did feel shame. He knew no other emotion in connection with failure. He did not want to add hurt to what Owen was already feeling.

"You're a good, hard worker and that will help to see you through."

That was probably the most difficult statement Owen ever had to make, to tell his parents he had failed, yet, therein was the source of the greatest encouragement. Mary and Griff had not lost their ability to influence their offspring to continue to aspire.

Their children did not have to know how they sat at the kitchen table lamenting— two divorces and a bankruptcy.

Chapter 42
༼ঌঌঌঌ

The following Christmas, Griff notified Mary that he did not feel good enough to go to any of the kids for the holiday. If any of them could come home that would be fine. This was alarming to Mary, because Griff had always liked to go when the opportunity arose. He would cough hard and long and was embarrassed by the commotion he caused. As Sarah looked over the Christmas pictures of her dad with her two grandsons, she commented on how frail and white he looked. Those were the last pictures taken of Griff.

It was back to the Sioux City hospital, this time by ambulance. Mary took up her boarding situation again and was with Griff until one afternoon she came home to get some clothes she needed. Sarah had come to take her back to visit her Dad, but the roads were too icy. They called him to let him know they would be there the next day. He sounded quite hearty over the phone. A few hours later, in the middle of the night, that dreaded phone call came. Husband and father, Griff was gone.

Mary experienced ambivalent feelings of being cheated and guilty at not being with Griff at his last breath. The ice was a genuine factor in her not being there. She had the bruises to prove it as she had fallen that evening. She had gotten up from that fall and after the immediate check to see if she was OK, it wasn't mentioned again. The reality of making funeral arrangements was demanding. Notifying relatives and seeing that the family could all stay at home. The thought of them staying in a motel was abhorrent to Mary. Of course the cemetery plot had been chosen long before by Griff when he said he'd like being in the shade of that tree. He did not know he would be buried on an extremely cold February day.

The three children and all the grandchildren were there in honor of their father and grandfather. This was a solace to Mary. They all comforted her, too, in confirming there were reasons she could not be with him when he died. A misprint in the obituary left out David's name as a son. This was disconcerting to Mary and Sarah, but David dealt with it in his manly way, "Don't stew over that, I know who I am." Sarah, although middle aged, never felt that she knew the right thing to say to a bereaved family. Now she knew that "I'm sorry" and a handshake were warmly comforting.

A dinner before and a lunch after the funeral were prepared by the Ladies' Aid. They knew how to function almost automatically once Mary gave them the signal of what she wanted and assured them that she would buy all the ham that was needed. Mary had been the planner of many such activities, and her mind worked clearly and efficiently throughout this time. To anyone who knew Mary, it was almost expected that she would do her grieving in this manner. When it came time to write the thank you notes, she rejected all family help. She wanted to do that personally. It was during this process that she dealt with the loss of that good man she called husband for fifty-four years.

Chapter 43
ᘓᗷᓚᔓ

Spring came again and Mary knew she could not leave the farm. Owen, Sarah, and David knew they could suggest to their mother what to do, but they could not rush her in making decisions. She would not sell the farm. That was an absolute. She sold the stock, turned over the pasture to the tenant, and switched to cash rent. This represented sound thinking. She tried keeping up the big front lawn.

"There is no reason I can't ride around on that mower as well as Griff did."

On one weekend Sarah visited and helped with the mowing. She was going up a little incline and the front of the mower raised and started to tip backwards. Sarah jumped off, the mower turned over, the wheels and blade were still going, she disengaged the gears and turned off the motor. She sat down on the front steps and shook with fear.

"It did that to me once. I know how you feel," Mary revealed.

"Mom, you just must not keep doing this. Someone is going to drive by someday and find you caught under that thing. I wouldn't get back on it for all the tea in China."

"Well, I'll see if I can get someone to do it." Mary conceded that much.

Sarah reasoned that it would not need many more mowings. She also planned a ride to the nearest towns to look around at what houses were available. She was hoping to plant the seeds of appeal of living in town. A long and snowy winter probably did more to move Mary to make that decision. She shopped and found a nice, smaller, newer home, handy to a grocery store. She could drive out to the country for Church, to Bridge Club and Woman's Club, except when the roads were bad. She got excited about the whole plan and went about it with enthusiasm.

The boys would come from Denver for the yard sale, and help move that same week. She relented and let the more youthful bodies do the hauling and putting things in place. Whenever she couldn't find something for years after, Mary's comment was, "We must have sold that at the sale."

She joined another bridge club in town, besides going to the Senior Citizen Center. The Ladies' Aid made special design quilts for lotteries which Mary supervised. Other old friends moved to town also. They laughed about the fact that so many from the home Church now lived there.

This group of stalwart women who had always accepted what life had brought them, were dealing with old age equally gracefully. Most of them were financially secure by their frugal practices and by husbands who wanted to be land owners. They were not in competition with each other. It was more of a gladness for each other.

Chapter 44
෬∾ఞ

Mary proved herself as an astute business woman. She added to their savings, and gave her children land and money. She made investments that made good interest. The kids expressed that they did not want her to sacrifice things that she wanted to give to them, but she insisted she had everything she wanted. She saved more than money. Scrapbooks had long been a fascination to her and now she had more time to sort and glue, while reading her past collections. Obituaries of everyone she had ever known were saved. These supplied a sort of personal reference library for the facts she wanted to know. She could remember just about where a certain article was glued on the page. Yet, she complained her memory wasn't very good. Her photo albums were equally interesting as they provided a family history. She crocheted afghans and read avidly. Her fine handwriting was always recognized in her correspondence, particularly with nieces and nephews whose parents were gone. All of Griff's siblings were deceased. Only two of the six of Mary's were still living. Mary, the oldest, the youngest and a middle sister were left. They had fine reunions before they were so few in number. Their memories were precious and they never doubted their common heritage when they heard their laughter. Mary never missed remembering a grandchild's or great grandchild's birthday.

In a writing class that Mary took, she was encouraged to write an autobiography. She had material for a lengthy treatise but not the energy. While probing into her past, these lines that follow came as an echo. She wrote them down revealing that young motherhood was a fulfilling aspect of her life.

All my life I've wished to do great things, like write a book or a song that everybody would sing. The years went by with little tasks. The ink dried and the paper stayed white. Fame still hidden, yet I starred. I had youthful arms embrace me. No fame or fortune can compare. Three happy children climbing on my knee. I'm content. Should the Master ask where are the talents that I gave you, I would answer my talents number three. My book and my song are their sweet smiles and voices happy and free.

Those talents three caused much heartache too. Through it all, there had been no family break. Communication was sustained. Mary knew that all she had done was not good and her children had made mistakes. She would have to scrutinize the status quo. Owen had survived the bankruptcy. His business was providing a living but not much future. He was not grim and despondent. Actually, he played the strong father role to his grown family. He was a warm and loving father and grandfather. Sarah had returned to education and in it found fulfillment and friendship. Time had healed and she would consider marriage again. She had thoughts of reconciling with Preston but his death intervened. She was a strong proponent of original families staying together. Life's experiences had given her growth in understanding, and her relationship with her daughters was rich. She became active in her church and community. David, like Sarah, did not rush back into marriage. The two siblings were close in spite of their years difference. They served as each other's confidante. David's business grew successfully. He accepted the advice of his older brother, "Don't get so big that you don't know what is going on and pay your taxes on time." He did not create a competitive situation between him and the mother of his children. They celebrated many holidays as a family. He never lost his place as the happy, fun-loving little brother, even though he was mature and caring.

Mary was comforted. The salt had not lost its savor.